THE TEN YEAR PLAN

THE TEN YEAR PLAN

JC Calciano

NYLA Publishing
350 7th Avenue, Suite 2003, NY 10001, New York.
http://www.nyliterary.com

Dedication

To my buddies - Michael and Brenton.

*If it weren't for their insanity and friendship
there would be no Myles and Brody.*

CHAPTER ONE

Myles Robertson was nervous – nothing new here – he was on the cusp of what could be the start of a happily ever after with Sam. He'd planned the evening meticulously, as always. They were in one of the fanciest restaurants Myles could find in Los Angeles: conversations at a low and intimate hum, softly lit and, of course, one of the most expensive. Nothing but the best tonight.

Out of sight, under the table, he held a red rose, anxious to be presented. He noticed Sam fidget and Myles furrowed his brow. He worried that he'd overlooked something that could ruin his plans… No, everything seemed fine, perfect even, though he did notice a tentative look in his date's eyes. Had he noticed Myles' worried state, his preoccupation with the situation? *Of course not,* Myles told himself. He was probably just as nervous.

At twenty-five years of age, Myles was slender, dark-haired, and classically handsome. His date was equally good-looking with hair of a lighter shade. Myles wore a maroon shirt with a white band in the collar, while the other man was dressed in a sports coat and open-neck shirt. Smart, casual, approachable. Their holiday cards would be adorable.

Myles fumbled with the rose under the table, juggling it from one hand to the other. With a twinkle in his eye, he glanced toward the waiter with a slight nod and a smile. It was time for champagne.

Ignoring the butterflies in his stomach, Myles pasted a wide grin on his face and stared into Sam's eyes. "Tonight is important," he said, "so I wanted to go somewhere special. Somewhere romantic. When you've met someone wonderful, you should spoil him, don't you think?"

Sam gave him a nervous but charming smile in return.

"It's important," he went on, "to find that special person who you can be yourself around. You know what I mean? Someone you feel you can spend the rest of your life with."

The waiter brought the champagne and winked. Myles picked up his glass. "This calls for a toast," he said, extending the glass. "Here's to relationships." He pulled out the rose. "For you." *Perfect,* he told himself. Absolutely perfect. Myles gave his date a heart-melting smile and cocked his head.

His date appeared overwhelmed as he raised his glass in return. "Here's to *first* dates."

They clinked glasses.

"Will you please excuse me?" the man asked setting down his glass and dabbing the corners of his mouth.

"Of course," Myles answered.

The other man stood and rushed toward the men's room. Bubbles had replaced the butterflies. And Myles, pleased with how things had gone, sat and enjoyed the moment. He'd nailed it, he thought. A perfect ten.

Then he had an inspiration. He pulled out his cell and began to text Sam. "Hi. Just wanted you to know I'm really enjoying our evening together." His smile became wider. "See you in a minute." He added a smiley face winking one eye. Sam had everything anyone could want in a man—personality, brains, rugged good looks and a winning smile. He had an MBA and a great job and was headed nowhere but up. *Yes!* Myles thought, he'd picked a winner.

Hands folded in front of him on the table, Myles waited for his date to return. He glanced at the other diners. Lovers, he could tell. Just like he and Sam were destined to be. He felt a warm glow engulfing his body. This is all he'd ever wanted. A sweet boyfriend he could love and spoil. Picking up his phone again, he couldn't wait to tell his best friend, Brody, how the evening was going.

...

Brody, a serious hunk, a jock with star quarterback looks, was on the verge of an amazing orgasm. He almost didn't hear his phone ring over the sound of the blood rushing in his ears, and the heavy breathing of the young hipster pinned beneath him that he'd met on Grindr just a little while ago. Through the haze, he recognized Myles' special ringtone and – speeding up his pace with several mighty thrusts – quickly came. Without thought or care that his partner finished off, Brody rolled over and picked up his cell from a nearby chair.

A giant, satisfied smirk crossed his face, the exact opposite of the disbelief on his partner's. "Hey, Myles. What's up?"

"He's cute and smart. I really like him. I think he may be the one."

Brody chuckled. He'd heard the same thing many times before. "What kind of puppy did you pick out?"

"Puppy?" Myles asked and Brody could visualize the wistful look on his face.

"The one you're imagining right now, with you in your dream house."

Myles laughed and played coy. "I have no idea what you're talking about." Then he paused and gushed, "Okay, a Boston Terrier." He quickly deflected and changed the subject. "Where are you, by the way? No, wait. Before you answer let me guess."

Brody's annoyed conquest got out of bed and headed to the bathroom naked, his perfect ass swaying gently as he walked.

"I'll give you two guesses, but I bet you don't need the second one." He made a sound between a purr and a growl as his eyes followed the beautiful stranger. "This guy's ass is so tight you could bounce a quarter off it... or something bigger."

Myles chuckled. "That's a nice visual to put in my head just before I enjoy my romantic dinner. My date and I are sharing a connection and having deep meaningful conversation. I took him to this amazing restaurant and just texted him in the bathroom to tell him that I miss him already."

Brody rolled his eyes. He knew this scenario all too well. "Bet he's hailing a cab, even as we speak" he chided.

Out of the corner of his eye, Myles caught Sam darting out of the restaurant's front door.

"No!" Myles sounded shocked.

"What is it?"

"Do you always have to be right?" a defeated Myles asked.

Brody swung his legs over the side of the bed. "I'm sorry?"

"What's wrong with me, Brody? Why is it they always dump me?"

"He left you?"

Myles signed deeply. "He just sneaked by; didn't think I saw him, I suppose. But I did."

"You saw him... what?"

"Sneaking past. Stepping outside, standing on the sidewalk, hailing a cab."

"Aw, Myles." He paused, not having thought the guy would actually bail on his friend. "Okay, tell me where you are." Brody pulled on his underwear and his jeans.

"Time to initiate our suicide pact?" Myles asked.

Brody couldn't help but smile when he imagined the accompanying gestures.

"I fear the time is upon us," Myles continued, his tone overly melodramatic. "Death by chocolate?"

"Meet you in ten minutes," Brody said as he clicked off his cell and looked at the young and chiseled hardbody standing before him, who'd walked back into the room. The young man held out a towel. "You owe me an orgasm."

"I'll make it a double next time," Brody answered, ignoring the towel.

"Will there be a next time?" He asked, not expecting a yes.

Brody looked him in the eye. "Probably not." At least he wasn't a liar, Brody thought as he pulled on his socks and shoes.

"No quick shower before you head out?"

Brody smiled mischievously. "No need. I didn't break a sweat." He checked his pockets to see if he had everything and headed toward the door. Suddenly, he had an idea that would require a stop at home before going to the restaurant. He had something he wanted to give Myles, but he knew he'd probably regret it... *Oh, what the hell,* he thought.

...

Brody Hamilton entered the restaurant carrying a small, wrapped package. On the way to the table where Myles sat, head drooping, he made eye contact with a young, tow-haired waiter with impossibly tight black pants, red apron, and a white shirt. He and the waiter exchanged quick and knowing glances.

"Nice place!" Brody said, as he pulled out the chair opposite his friend and sat down.

Myles looked up. "At least it was before my date left."

On the table sat two slices of chocolate cake and an ice-cold beer. He smiled. "Well you certainly know what I like."

"I suppose we know as much about each other as anyone does."

Brody gave a slight shrug and handed him the package. "Maybe this will help cheer you up."

"What's this for?" he asked.

"It's for you."

Myles rolled his eyes. "I assumed that. What I mean is—"

"It's your birthday present."

"Birthday present. Brody…"

"Yes?"

"You know my birthday's not for another two months."

"Well, the way I figured it is that now's the time you could use a little bit of 'happy'. And, of course, I'll get you something else on your actual birthday. Anyhow, don't get excited. It's really nothing."

As neat as ever—a real Felix in *The Odd Couple* way—Myles carefully untied the small red ribbon and unwrapped what lay beneath. He looked astounded as tears glistened in his eyes. It was a framed photo of Myles and Brody on the day they met.

Uh oh, Brody thought. Tears. Just what he was afraid of. "Come on," he said, "don't get all gushy on me."

Myles gave him a tender smile. "Ah," he said, "a chink in the armor. You do have a sentimental side!"

"I made two of them. One for you and one for me."

"I knew you were just a big softy."

"No!" The word sounded harsh. "No, Myles. I just knew you'd like it. Don't make me regret doing something nice for you."

"Uh huh."

"Okay. Enough sappy crap. A toast!" He raised the bottle of beer. "To guys. Fuck 'em."

Myles held up his glass to return the toast. "To friends; to relationships."

"To being single," Brody countered and raised the bottle to his lips.

Myles sighed. He realized he and Brody were on totally different pages in their lives. Yet he was determined to make the toast that he wanted to make. "To finding the perfect man."

"To friends," Brody snapped.

"To relationships!"

"To being single!"

They both laughed and downed their respective drinks.

Myles gazed at Brody and thought of life without him. "Do me a favor," he said. "Don't let me die alone?"

Brody laughed, "You certainly won't be alone. I'll be there holding the pillow over your face! Another toast!" Again, he raised the bottle. "To the hangovers we'll have tomorrow!" They clink glass and bottle and take another swallow.

"So we agree?" Myles said.

"To being hung over tomorrow?"

"No. That we won't grow old alone." The tone of his voice was more serious now.

The waiter returned to fill their water glasses, brushing against Brody and pressing his crotch against Brody's shoulder. He finished filling the water glasses and lingered a bit too long.

Myles shot him a look that clearly said, "Back off."

Brody, on the other hand, grinned impishly. With a slight toss of his head the waiter retreated, Brody staring at his sexy ass. It was obvious the waiter knew he was being watched.

Myles shook his head, making Brody laugh.

Maybe he had no right to be jealous, Myles thought, but nevertheless he was. Of course, it was only his stupid obsessive-compulsive fear of becoming a spinster.

"You're worried about being alone, aren't you?"

Myles shrugged.

"I'm never alone," Brody answered. "In fact, I'm already drafting up a list in my head. All those things I plan on doing to our cute waiter. Most, if not all, are still illegal in forty-two states."

"Please, Brody, I'm serious."

"You know I'll always be there for you. In fact, I can tell you're already obsessing about this." He shook his head and grinned. "Tell you what. I'll make you a deal. If we're both single ten years from now and neither of us has found anyone, we'll be together. Boyfriends. A couple. Together. Forever."

Myles was baffled. "Are you being serious?"

Brody grabbed a small drink napkin from the empty table next to them along with the pen that the previous couple had left behind, no doubt after signing their credit card slip. "You're the fancy attorney. Write it, I'll sign it. Make it legally binding."

Myles' face lit up like an amber spotlight. "So I have ten years?"

"Yes. Ten years to find love, before you turn thirty-five."

Myles held up his drink in celebration. He'd finally succeeded in getting Brody to commit to something. "Here's to being in love."

Brody shook his head. "To ten more years of freedom."

Myles scrawled a few sentences on the napkin, signed it, and handed it to Brody, who read it quickly and scribbled his name next to Myles' signature. They toasted.

Myles couldn't believe it. Why had Brody done this? Brody, the perpetual bachelor. Maybe he was counting on Myles having a relationship by then. Or maybe he'd just try to back out. Or more to the point, he was trying to be a supportive friend but he'd just throw the napkin away later. Well, at least he could prevent that. He reached over to take the napkin back.

"Nope, can't have it," Brody told him as he stuck it into his pants pocket, unworried. What were the odds a guy like Myles would still be single in ten years?

CHAPTER TWO

Nine years, ten months, and twenty-nine days later:

Myles scurried from the kitchen to the dining room table and back again, anxious, as usual, to make sure that everything was just right. Of course, it was. Everything was always in its rightful place Myles' house—as clean and neat as an operating room, if not so sterile looking, almost like a home décor magazine photo shoot was going to happen any minute.

On the couch sat a young man simply observing. Kodi, a frat boy type, with good clothes and a solid frame watched with an amazed look on his face as Myles, like a rat in a maze, hurried here and there, adding little touches to the table. He watched as Myles ensured the plates and silverware lined up exactly, and then appear to look over the settings for the fifth time, at least. If he had brought out a ruler to check the table Kodi wouldn't have been surprised.

"Don't you ever slow down?" Kodi asked. Just looking at Myles exhausted him.

"In a moment," Myles answered. After ten years he hadn't changed much, except that he seemed a little more confident. Maybe it was the result of his financial success, reflected in the fine furnishings and objects d'art that occupied his living and dining areas. The romantic music providing the carefully crafted ambience of the evening played on a high tech sound system. Myles himself wore a crisp pressed, striped apron that complemented his grey shirt perfectly.

Once more he entered the dining room, now carrying a tray filled with a collection of exotic meats—venison, goose nuggets, caribou sausage—mushroom and walnut paté, and various cheeses. A bottle of fine wine sat in front of Kodi.

"Hey, Babe. I made you those appetizers you like with imported goat cheese and caviar, but don't eat too many!"

"What?" Totally overwhelmed, Kodi couldn't keep up with Myles. "I said—"

"I heard what you said. I just—" It was obvious Kodi wanted to say more but couldn't get another word in and fidgeted on the couch.

"I cooked something extra special." He glanced at Kodi, so caught up in unveiling the perfect evening that he missed the nerves play across his date's face. "And you don't want you to ruin that appetite of yours."

"Myles. Relax. Please. Sit down!"

"In a minute. Trust me, you don't want dinner to burn!"

The rich aroma of Myles' cooking had been filling the apartment slowly and Kodi drew back and took a deep breath, looking transfixed. Myles hurried once more to the kitchen and came back holding a wooden spoon heaped with food. "It's eggplant Sorrento," Myles said. "I know it's your favorite."

"How could you possibly...?" Kodi's voice trailed off as he tried to puzzle out some reasonable explanation.

"I called your mother to ask what you like; she gave me the recipe."

"Are you kidding me? You're making my mom's Eggplant Sorrento?"

Myles beamed, thrilled he could do something this wonderful for his boyfriend. "You've been working a lot, so I thought it would be nice to do something special for you."

"I can't believe you called my mother. That's a tad scary."

Myles' nerves gave a jolt but he kept on talking. "Please, just relax. Take your shoes off and drink up. It's an '86 Cabernet. I'll be back in a few." Myles quickly filled Kodi's glass and was once more off to the kitchen.

...

Meanwhile, Brody, muscular and hotter than ever, and his partner Richard, a sexy, forty-year-old Latino with a wrestler's build, were at the police station changing out of their uniforms into civilian clothes. Other cops swarmed through the locker room in various stages of undress.

"Hey, partner," Richard said, "wanna catch a movie tonight? I'll buy the popcorn... again."

Brody wrapped a towel around his waist as he headed toward the shower. "Sorry, bud," he called over his shoulder, "but I got plans. They start with a beer and they end with a sticky towel." He gave his partner a wicked grin.

Richard chuckled in self-deprecation as he held up his hand. "Looks like it's just you and me again tonight, buddy."

Brody turned back toward his partner. "Hey, you're the one who insists on being straight. Come out with me tonight. I guarantee that in ten minutes I'll hook you up with an ass you can eat breakfast, lunch, and dinner off of!"

"Sorry, but I prefer my partners not have the same equipment as me."

Brody chuckled. "Not me." He held up a shoe in preparation of putting it on. "I prefer the same or bigger." He shrugged. "Well, it's your loss."

Just then Brody's Grindr app chimed. He picked up his cell and checked it out. "Oooo. Very nice!" He showed Richard the screen. "Meet David."

The man appeared to be in his mid twenties with an Ivy League look—like a hot college stud taking a shirtless selfie in the mirror. He had blond hair and an almost cherubic face. Hello, new plans.

Richard shook his head, mostly at his own lack of luck with women of late. "Is it really that easy for you?"

"That's the great thing about men. No wining and dining them. In five minutes I'll have had a beer. In fifteen minutes, we'll be in the sack. Sixty minutes later I'll be home watching a movie on pay-per-view. It's pretty great. You should try it."

Richard paused for a moment. "It does sound tempting... and since you put it that way..."

Brody face brightened. He couldn't believe he'd finally recruited his hot Mexican partner! Almost too easy. "Really? You'll do it?!"

Richard laughed hard. "Hell no!"

They broke into raucous laughter when the other cops looked at them and rolled their eyes, used to the duos antics.

Growing up, Richard was always popular with the ladies. He was strong and muscular and, of course, his "Latin lover" good looks. His darker skin, broad shoulders, and square jaw guaranteed he was never want for attention from the fairer sex. And due to his size and appearance, people naturally respected his presence. He had a cool, collected calm about him that reassured others. Everyone knew he could "take care of business" if it came to it, so it rarely ever did.

Though he looked like a rock from the outside, on the inside, Richard had the sensitivity of a poet and the thoughtfulness of a priest. A Hallmark card could choke him up. Ads on TV about boys and their fathers made his eyes misty. And though he would never admit it to his buddies, he loved watching romance movies and romantic comedies, even more than any of the summer blockbusters or thrillers, the movies he watched with them.

Richard came from a line of lawmen—following in his grand-father's and father's footsteps. He truly believed in the slogan: To serve and protect.

Though Richard was only a few years older than Brody, he was the veteran. They were assigned to work together not long after Richard's former partner retired. It was his responsibility to teach Brody the ropes, show him around the precinct and initiate him into the force.

The first step was drinks out with his fellow officers. Brody could handle his liquor, which was always a good sign. It showed he had some real stamina. The next step was watching football and basketball games together, along with some afternoon barbeques with the other guys. And last but never least, strip clubs. Richard worked hard every day and on his nights off he played hard too.

And that was the start of Brody and Richard's friendship.

. . .

"As Time Goes By" from *Casablanca* played softly in the background. The gas fireplace hissed along; lights were turned down low.

Myles knew Kodi didn't drink much. So the half empty bottle of wine in front of him tipped off the fact that something was wrong. But Myles didn't want to acknowledge there could be a problem. Maybe Kodi was just tired. After all he'd had a big meeting today, and that could wear anyone out. He held out a spoonful of Eggplant Sorrento. "Someone was hungry. And thirsty!" he said as he moved the spoon closer to Kodi's face. "Here, taste."

"Are you going to sit down? I'd really like to talk to you..." He tried to catch Myles' eyes to get him to slow down for just a second, but Myles was too excited about sharing his culinary creation and thrust the piping hot food into Kodi's mouth.

Kodi's eyes lit up.

"Wow. That's amazing! It's exactly like my mother makes it!"

Success! That's all Myles wanted to hear. He was proud of being the perfect boyfriend and excited about being one step closer to Kodi's finally being "the one."

"I'm so pleased! Now, I want to hear all about your day. Come to the table. We'll talk over dinner!"

Myles headed to the table as Kodi had one last gulp of wine and then took a deep breath as if to prepare himself for something unpleasant.

. . .

Brody pulled up to David's house, a little Hollywood bungalow. It had been a long day, and a quick no-strings-attached fuck sounded like the perfect way to kick off the evening. Brody hoped David looked as good in person as he did in his photos. He was in no mood to be greeted by someone who posted another person's photos on Grindr or used a picture that was ten years old.

He rang the bell and hoped for the best. Seconds later, the door opened. Wow. Not only did David look much like the photo on the website but somehow even better. Through the snug shirt he was wearing, Brody could see the sculpted body of a gymnast. Perfectly tight muscles, a strong sculpted "v" torso and a shirt just short enough to reveal a trail of golden hair leading down the front of his jeans. Brody smiled. This was going to be fun. At first glance David was a delicious treat waiting to be gobbled up.

"Hi. I'm David," he said, with a hint of hesitation in his voice. It was obvious he was a virgin at this sort of thing and was terrified.

That's probably his real name, Brody thought, though he really couldn't condemn him for that. He was young and didn't know the rules of the game most of the guys played yet. Brody used his own name too. It was simpler, rather than trying to remember which pseudonym he used with which men. Brody gave him a mocking grin. "Hi. I'm Brody."

"It's nice to meet you," he said with a nervous laugh. And then he stood there. Awkwardly.

Brody laughed at the exchange. "Let me ask you: why is it guys always introduce themselves at the door like I don't know who they are by now? You've already sent me so many photos of yourself that I know you better than your doctor does."

"I don't know," he said, suddenly insecure with himself, "Do you have a better way of greeting someone at the door?"

"How about this: Hey, Brody, come in. Would you like a beer?"

David looked momentarily startled and then smiled. "Hi, Brody, come in. Would you like a beer?"

Brody chuckled. "Nah. I'm good. But thanks for asking." He stepped inside with a confident stride. "You look terrified, David. First time using Grindr?"

"No." He grimaced. "Maybe." He glanced into Brody's eyes. "Yeah."

An innocent, fresh young stud, Brody thought. What could be better? Or cuter? "Everything's going to be okay, David," he said. "We'll have fun tonight. Don't worry."

David turned and Brody followed him. "How about you, David? Can I get you a beer?"

David suddenly relaxed.

Brody was glad. He looked like a good guy. And, oh, so hot. "Actually. I'd love one."

David welcomed him inside as he headed to the kitchen to get that beer. Brody followed him. Their evening had begun.

The kitchen was dark as David opened the refrigerator door, his torso outlined by the weak light emanating from inside. He twisted the cap from a bottle and took a long deep swallow. Brody could almost imagine the cold brew sliding down David's parched throat, his body relaxing as he swallowed. He realized the man needed a beer to calm his nerves and felt sorry for him, yet at the same time amused. Had he himself ever been so naive and innocent?

"Ahh," David said releasing a pent up breath, his shoulders relaxed.

"Feel better?" Brody asked.

David smiled and nodded. "I really needed that."

"Besides," Brody said, "the cold air from the fridge feels good on a hot night like this." Of course, it was a double entendre.

"Sure I can't get you that beer? You know there's nothing better than a cold beer on a hot night."

"Well, there's one thing that's better."

"And what might that be?" David answered coyly, his eyes roamed slowly over Brody's body.

"I have only one question for you David... what's your safe word?"

"What?!"

Brody could see he had scared the other man. "I'm just playing with you."

David visibly relaxed and tried to grin. "Guess you got me," he said.

"Tell you what," Brody said. "Since this is your first time... I'll be gentle. For the first hour, anyhow!" He stepped toward David.

David took another long gulp of beer but not before Brody slid his hand down the front of David's jeans. David was hard from the moment Brody touched him. "What do they put in the feed in those mid-western towns?" Brody asked. "They certainly grow you farm boys big!"

David blushed, embarrassed yet obviously enjoying what Brody was doing. "I'm not exactly a farm boy," he answered.

"Not exactly?'

"From a small town in Michigan."

"Ah, explains it," Brody answered jokingly, "All that clean air."

Brody leaned forward and pressed his soft lips against David's mouth, tasting the beer on his tongue. The two men continued to kiss as Brody gently squeezed David's cock. He was surprised to feel it growing even larger. Brody took the beer from David's hand and finished it with a mighty gulp. Foreplay was over.

...

Candles flickered on the table; plates were picked clean. Myles had outdone himself.

"Oh, man, Myles," Kodi said, "I should never admit it. But this was even better than what Mom makes." He patted his stomach and accidentally belched. Quickly, he covered his mouth in embarrassment and blushed.

Myles was flattered. Best way to compliment the cook, after all.

"How did the meeting go with your client?" Myles asked, trying to break the tension.

Kodi didn't say anything. He just sat for a moment staring into Myles' face, as if trying to decide what to do.

Myles felt a tinge of alarm, tried to stop the waves of nerves that rolled over him, and then quickly continued. "I hope you got all the 'I'm-thinking-of-you' texts I sent."

Myles could tell Kodi felt uneasy, as if he were about to apologize for something. Myles didn't know what. His answer wasn't what Myles expected.

"Yup, I got all ten of them." His tone was sarcastic.

Suddenly, things were coming into focus, and Myles realized he'd been deluding himself. The evening wasn't going the way he hoped it would. Still, he tried to redeem things. Elbows on the table, he leaned forward. "You seem a little... tired? Maybe if you take your shoes off. Relax a little. Stay for a while."

Kodi looked stone-faced. That was when Myles began to realize that as usual, he'd tried too hard. Things had been too perfect—the wine, the appetizers, the music, the glow from the fireplace.

"I'm fine. Really." He sat stiffly. "I'm just trying to figure out the best way to talk to you about something."

Myles didn't know how to react. Obviously the dinner conversation was turning into one that was all too familiar? It was the same conversation, with slight variations, that he'd had with a dozen men before Kodi. He mustered up a nervous smile, "As long as it's not, 'let's see other people.'"

Kodi's drawn face looked impassive. Clearly Miles had hit the nail on the head and he sighed. "You want to see other people?" His voice sounded resigned.

Kodi tried to soften the blow. "I'm thinking we're going too fast."

"We've been dating a month, and I see you once a week for dinner and sex. And I do all the work for both. How is that going too fast?"

Koki looked uncomfortable, so much so that Myles almost felt sorry for him. Almost.

"I just want to pump the brakes a bit."

Myles was dying inside. He could almost literally feel that last tiny spark of hope he held onto start to flicker and die in his chest. He couldn't believe this was happening. Not again. What was he doing that was so wrong? Trying to see that everything went well? Making sure the evening was successful. Myles shook his head. Kodi had seemed right for him. Suddenly, Myles was irritated.

"Maybe you could have pumped them on a day that I didn't spend cooking an elaborate dinner and planning erotic massages?" He stood and opened the bedroom door behind him and then turned back.

Kodi's face dropped at the sight of a bedroom full of candles and a massage table. Fresh cut flowers stood on the dresser and chest of drawers. Incense burned in tiny saucers.

"Wow, Myles. That's incredible. Really. All I can say is that one day you are going to make someone the most amazing husband."

He finally accepted the situation. "Just not you?"

Kodi stood and for a moment stared into Myles' eyes, a look close to regret on his face, "No," he said softly, "I'm going to leave." He opened the door, quietly slipped out into the hallway, and away from Myles' happily ever after.

Myles slumped in his chair, elbows on the table, chin rested in his hands. What had he done wrong this time?

. . .

Brody lay in David's bed, relaxed, their bodies glistening with sweat. Brody smiled as he grabbed David's tee shirt and wiped semen from his abs. David lay back, watching. Brody gently kissed his lips as he tossed the cum-soaked tee shirt onto the floor. He felt like a cat that had eaten a chocolate-covered mouse.

"That was certainly fun," Brody said. "Did you enjoy it?" The answer was obvious. All Brody needed to do was look under the sheets.

"Oh yeah! Hey, can I get you a beer now?"

"You're a quick study, David. I like you."

"Enough to see me again?"

Brody laughed. He'd set the hook in this one. He knew that David was his for the taking any time he wanted. But it was better to not let him think this was going to be anything more than what it was. Being friends with a romantic like Myles didn't do his conscience any favors.

"I like you enough to introduce you to my best friend."

David looked unsure. "A threesome? I don't know if I'm ready for that yet..."

"Sure you are!" Brody picked up his phone.

. . .

Myles sat at the dining room table, too defeated to clean up.

His cell phone rang, snapping him out of his funk. It was Brody face-timing him. He smiled. *This is really the only man I want to be with tonight,* he thought. Brody looked spectacular as always, and suddenly the evening sucked less.

"Myles. Meet David."

Myles realized Brody was lying next to another man. Insult upon injury. Of course Brody was on the prowl. Once more the evening completely sucked. But Brody was his friend, so he'd put on his game face. "Hello, David. It's always a pleasure meeting one of Brody's 'friends', especially just after I've been dumped."

Brody rolled his eyes, but his face held a look of sympathy. "Want me to come over?"

Myles smiled. Of course, that was what he wanted. "That depends. Do you like strawberries infused with cognac hand dipped in dark chocolate?"

Brody chuckled.

Myles was aware that David was witnessing the exchange.

"Strawberries and cognac?" David asked. "Can I come?"

Without missing a beat Brody turned to him. "You already did. Twice."

They both laughed, then Brody turned his attention back to the phone, spouted off a quick, "I'll be right there" and hung up.

David was confused when Brody slipped his jeans on, but the look on both Myles' and Brody's faces when they saw each other made it clear. David was no competition for Myles' attention. Besides, David had gotten what he wanted and more. He certainly wasn't going to complain. It was best that the evening ended this way.

Brody kissed David deeply. "Thanks."

"For what?"

Brody laughed. "For being a good guy; for looking like your photo."

"And?" David was being coy.

"I'm sure you know," Brody said. "But okay, I'll say it. For the evening; it was great." Brody meant it, but still nothing made him feel better than knowing he was going to see his best friend.

. . .

Brody noticed that everything looked absolutely flawless. Myles didn't even have a hair out of place, and the apartment looked just as perfect. They sat at the still decked out table and Brody couldn't help himself. "Since when did you start fucking Martha Stewart?" There was a twinkle in his eye.

"One does what one has to, to get a man," Myles answered. His tone was joking but the smile didn't quite reach his eyes.

"Well, I've had a lot of men, and I've never once injected a strawberry with cognac. Well, not in the literal sense." They both chuckled at the naughty turn of phrase.

Then Myles thought of the disastrous evening he'd just endured and felt worse than ever. "It doesn't matter anyway. I'm done. I'm in my mid-thirties. Time to acknowledge the fact that I'm destined to be a gay spinster. If the thought of dog hair everywhere didn't disgust me, I'd be a gay cliché."

"Trust me, you don't need the small dog to be a gay cliché."

"Thank you so much." He gave Brody a look of mock irritation. "Either way, I'm tired and done. I'm finished chasing men only to have my heart broken every time."

Brody had to do something; he didn't know exactly what. He couldn't stand to see Myles put himself through the wringer like this. Maybe if he made Myles do something different, got him out of his comfort zone. What could he do? Hmmm. Well, what about a sex store? He was sure Myles had never been to one. He could just see his reaction—the guy who never did anything new.

It might be fun too. "Come on," he told Myles, "you need a little shopping spree. If you're going to be single, you're going to need the proper tools, and I know exactly where to get them!"

Myles could detect Brody's mischievous grin a mile away. He knew he was up to no good and the night would take them to a crazy and unfamiliar place. Myles knew he needed a bit of fun, and Brody was the man for the job. He smiled and braced himself for what he knew would be a new adventure.

CHAPTER THREE

Brody led Myles into Chi Chi Larue's, an adult toyshop on Santa Monica Blvd. Chi Chi herself was widely known as the queen of gay porn. Techno music pulsated; purple and pink light bathed a sea of dildos, videos and various sex toys that were beyond Myles' comprehension.

Brody on the other hand was a regular.

"What are you getting me into?" Myles shouted above the music.

Brody ignored him, his eyes already surveying the aisles.

Myles has never been in such a place before. Of course, he had known they existed but not to this extent! Yet Brody had entered as casually as another person might enter a Starbucks for morning coffee. To Myles it seemed surreal—the music, the abundance of "toys", the porn books and magazines. If Brody wanted to shock him, he'd succeeded. Myles let his gaze wander here and there. *Astounding,* he thought. He couldn't process it all, couldn't even imagine what a lot of the things he saw were for. It boggled his mind.

Brody headed straight for the toys and then turned to Myles. "If I know you, an evening of kinky sex means using your left hand. And your toy arsenal is nothing more than a two-year old jar of lube."

Myles felt amused and only slightly annoyed that Brody was right.

"Being single requires the proper equipment, and there's no better place to get it than here!" Brody picked up cylinder with a mouth attached to it. It was a "fleshjack". He handed it to his friend. "Here you go. Better than a real mouth. Why? Because it doesn't speak!" He cracked himself up.

Next up was a large sculpted dildo, modeled after porn-star Jeff Stryker's cock. "Take this... so there's no more gambling with what's on the other side of the zipper." He glanced into Myles' eyes. "Let's be honest. No one likes to unwrap the whopper only to find they skimped on the pickle." He held thumb and finger a couple of inches apart. "Now you can come home to Jeff Stryker every night."

Obviously, Myles was impressed but also a bit horrified by the size of the silicon cock. It looked more like a bludgeon than a sex toy.

Brody continued. "Mini projector for the bedroom ceiling. You can watch your favorite pornos in wide-screen above you."

Myles shook his head. "One can see you've done extensive research on the subject of sex."

"I only know how to do a few things. But... the things I'm good at, I'm an expert on."

Brody filled a basket with the toys. When they turned, they were face to face with Chi Chi.

"So good to see you again, honey," she purred to Brody. "Looks like you two boys are in for one hell of a night."

"Oh! No, no," Myles answered. "This isn't for us. We're just friends. It's all for me."

Brody and Chi Chi just stared at Myles for a moment. Myles felt his face turn red. In the effort to prevent a misunderstanding he'd made matters worse! Brody tried to contain his smile as he watched Myles' face turn bright red.

"Ooo," Chi Chi growled deep in her throat. "Aren't you the little tiger?" She clawed the air seductively.

Brody didn't bother hiding his laughter that time.

"Well, I'm not going to use it all tonight. Who could?" Myles laughed uncomfortably.

Brody and Chi Chi shared another look but seemed to come to an agreement not to say anything.

At the cash register, a still red-faced Myles pulled out his wallet.

"Uh uh," Brody said, "it's on me. Consider it your 'singles emergency kit'."

Myles usually felt uncomfortable when Brody wanted to pay for anything, and it often led to a dispute. But this time he let it go. Yes, Myles made vastly more money than a regular cop, but Brody was by no means starving. Besides, Myles thought, he could never justify spending his money on this sort of thing, and it did seem important to Brody. Why not try something new?

Back at his apartment building Myles thanked Brody and promised him he'd be all right.

"Now look," Brody told him in a flirtatious tone, "if you need instructions on any of the toys, give me a call."

"I'm sure I won't," Myles said dryly and shook his head and waved as Brody drove off.

Back in his apartment, he set down his goody bag from Chi Chi's. Myles smiled ear to ear. Who knew such a terrible night could end up being so much fun? The dirty dishes and remnants from the latest break up still cluttered the dining room table. He knew he'd never be able to sleep with this mess left behind. Besides, he wanted all evidence of a bad evening stricken from the record. Dishes washed, candles put away and linens in the washing machine. Everything was almost as it was before his last date with Kodi. After clearing the table he grabbed the bowl of strawberries. He smiled thinking about Brody's being there to support him. As different as they were from each other, Brody had always been a great friend when the chips were down. He might sometimes show up late and hungover, but he would show.

Myles ate the last strawberry and thought, not bad. Not bad at all. He put the bowl in the dishwasher along with the silverware and dirty dishes. Next he straightened the place mats and made sure everything was back the way it should be.

In his bedroom, he hid the new toys in his bedside table. *Baby steps,* he thought. Myles undressed but before getting in bed took a look at himself in the mirror. He turned left and then right. "Kodi doesn't know what he missed tonight," he said aloud.

He pulled back the sheets and climbed under the covers. A quick video on the iPad would might do him some good. He was a little wound up after his trip with Brody. Maybe a few episodes of "Steam Room Stories" on You Tube? They always put a smile on his face. Hot boys doing silly sketch comedy, why not? Either that or a Food Network cooking show. He finally decided on the latter—a cooking show. No need to get himself worked up again watching sexy men. He'd had enough of that for the evening. Brody in Chi Chi Larue's definitely bordered on things Myles' should not be replaying in his head this late at night.

. . .

Brody handed the food truck vendor a twenty and told him to keep the change. The sun was shining, birds chirping. *Beautiful Los Angeles,* Brody thought. Another day in paradise. He and Richard grabbed their tacos and sat on the hood of their cruiser, both in full uniform. Another day on the job as LA's finest.

"I can't believe you make me eat here," Richard complained, not that it stopped him from shoving the food into his mouth.

Brody rolled his eyes. Richard didn't like to try new things, and food trucks weren't excluded. "Are you kidding? Everyone knows the best food in LA comes from food trucks."

"Yeah, so does e coli." He took another bite and then turned toward his partner. "I'm Mexican. I know how this is made!"

Brody chuckled. "Admit it; it's delicious, and this is my new favorite spot, so you're just going to have to deal with it." Brody reached into his pocket and pulled out what looked like a plastic egg. "Hey, Myles and I went toy shopping last night. I got you something. It's a sex toy."

Richard took it and looked it over. "If this goes where I think it does, you and I are about to have a problem, partner."

Brody laughed. "It doesn't. It's a sleeve you use to cover your junk when you jerk off. Just trust me on this. You'll like it. It feels amazing—better than the real thing."

Richard looked at him as to say, "Really? Better than the real thing?"

Brody knew he was probably thinking about boundaries and how Brody ignored them. Well, Brody was honest about it. Not everyone could handle this sort of thing, but Richard could. This was one of the things that made him choose Brody as a partner years earlier.

Brody could read his expression like a third grade textbook. He and Richard were great partners and friends. There wasn't anything that Brody didn't know about Richard and vice versa. Two men who had been partners on the force as long as they were and who spent whatever free time they both had together were inevitably going to form a bond—almost as strong as the bond Brody had with Myles.

He responded to Richard's look, "Of course not as good as the real thing, but definitely a close second and certainly better than your hand!"

Richard just shook his head.

"I took Myles shopping to try to cheer him up. He just broke up with his newest boyfriend. I bought him a bunch of toys and thought I'd pick you up a little something too," Brody said.

"Myles broke up with another one? I feel so bad for that guy."

"Me too, Myles is a bit much."

"No. I meant Myles."

Brody was surprised. "You feel bad for Myles? Don't! If you want to pity someone, try me. Myles and I made a deal ten years ago that if we were single by the time we're thirty-five, we'd be a couple! What am I going to do?"

Richard laughed. "That's ridiculous. Myles is a successful, smart lawyer. He can do so much better than you!"

"Right. I... What?"

Richard got a cheap shot in at Brody, who was surprised yet pleased at Richard's cleverness. Brody's sense of humor definitely was rubbing off on him.

"Besides, I don't know what you're complaining about. I think it's a great idea. You'd be lucky to be with someone like Myles."

The surprise turned to shock. Was Richard kidding? For someone who was supposed to know him well, Brody was amazed at how wrong he was. Well, just chalk it up to his being hetero. What did straight guys know about gay men anyhow? Richard was way off in the weeds on this one! "Absolutely not. That's the last thing in the world I need! Myles turns thirty-five in a month. That means we have thirty days to find him a new boyfriend so I'm off the hook!"

"Not us, my friend. Just you. I'm not getting involved in this."

"What?"

"Dum, dum, de dum," Richard sang. "Here comes the bride."

"That's not funny!"

Richard couldn't stop laughing. "Are you sure... because I think it's hysterical!"

...

Brody and Richard drove along Santa Monica Boulevard. When time permitted, Brody loved to drive cut through WeHo. Not just for the sake of checking out the guys walking along the street but to drive Richard a little nuts as well. It was the little things in life that meant so much sometimes.

"Now that is one cute little boy there in shorts and flip flops," Brody said with a grin.

"Why do you always do this to me? Just once I'd love to check out the ladies on Melrose shopping for short skirts and tight t-shirts," Richard moaned.

"Learn to enjoy the best of both worlds."

"I'd rather enjoy a nice ass in tight jeans."

"We have those too."

"A girl's ass, please."

Brody laughed. "All right, I've probably tortured you enough for one day. You can't blame me for trying."

Richard shook his head. He knew Brody's routine all too well.

"I'll cut down to Melrose so you can…"

Richard interrupted and got serious, "Hold on second."

Brody could hear it in his partner's voice. Something wasn't quite right.

"Over there," he pointed at two suspicious looking men wearing long coats on a summer's day walking into a convenience store. One of the man's wrists had a pair of handcuffs hanging from it.

"I see 'em," Brody replied.

He quickly pulled the squad car to the curb. The two of them hopped out and cautiously moved to the side of the store. Brody carefully peaked in the window. He could see the clerk staring uncomfortably at the two men. They were doing all the talking as the clerk listened–his eyes wide. The clerk, a man in his early sixties, pointed nervously towards the back of the store. One of the men indicated "move" with his head. They followed the clerk towards the back but not before glancing at the front door to make sure the coast was clear.

"It looks like we have a 211," Brody said.

"I'll call it in," Richard replied. He clicked on his walkie-talkie mike clipped to his shirt. "Dispatch, this is 98. We have a 211 in progress at Franklin's Hardware. Request back up."

"This is Dispatch, 98. Back up on the way."

Brody looked at Richard. They nodded. No time to wait for back-up.

Guns drawn, they entered the hardware store slowly and quietly; then the bell above the door tinkled loudly. The two cringed. They couldn't believe their luck.

Brody indicated with his head, *got to go now!*

They spread out and started systematically moving through the store, each time peaking down the next aisle cautiously. Brody spotted the three men talking at the back. The man with the handcuffed wrist was gesturing wildly. The clerk was still wide-eyed.

"I need this off my wrist right now," blurted the man with the handcuffs. He turned to his partner in crime, "What if I'm seen?"

His accomplice talked quickly, "We're going to need money."

"I understand. I just don't want anyone to get hurt," the clerk nervously replied.

"Freeze!" shouted Brody. "Hands up and where we can see them. Right now."

The three men turned to find Brody and Richard pointing their guns at them.

The second of the two men let out a yelp and fell backwards hitting a large stack of paint cans knocking them to the floor. As he flopped about, Brody and Richard could see his trench coat had come open. He was wearing nothing but shoes and black leather underwear, which had a policeman's badge, stitched into the crotch area. Brody and Richard stared at the men for a second and then lowered their guns.

The man with the handcuffs on his wrist kept his arms high in the air. His trench coat had come undone as well. He had on prison orange boxers with "Inmate–City Jail" printed on them. It was simply a case of role-playing gone wrong.

The older clerk stood wide-eyed holding a small hacksaw. He looked as if he peed in his pants. Well, actually he had.

Ten minutes later Brody and Richard were at the front of the store talking to four other officers, their backup, who shook their heads in disbelief. The two "suspects" had wanted to spice their love life up and had visited Chi Chi Larue's the day before and picked up some new toys and costumes. It was a case of cops & robbers gone bad when then men realized they not only had lost the handcuff keys somewhere in the yard, but they were now also locked out of their own house with no way to get back in and very little to wear. The cashier at the nearby Out of the Closet thrift shop had been kind enough to lend them two overcoats so they could get help to remove the handcuffs from the local locksmith at the hardware store. The backup officers tried to hold back their laughter in front of the two distraught men, but it wasn't easy.

At the front counter, the clerk continued to try to saw the handcuffs off the "inmate's" wrist while his still shaken partner held his coat closed tight around his body and tried to calm his nerves. Brody was sure they'd never try something like this again and thought, that's one way to make sure their sex life stayed vanilla.

...

Brody was going to pick up Myles and go to a bar for happy hour—something he'd been looking forward to so much that he didn't stop at the station to change. Today proved to be an exceptionally hard one. After the incident at the hardware store the other officers on the force were relentless. Brody knew he deserved all the ribbing they gave him; he would have given it to them should the circumstances been reversed. Still he was tired; he needed a drink and to simply sit and bullshit with a buddy. He parked in front of Myles' place and knocked on the door. Funny, he thought, but the house felt more like home than his own apartment. He knocked a second time.

"It's open."

Brody walked inside. As usual, OCD Myles was tidying up, making sure everything was where it should be. Myles—wearing grey slacks and a pale blue shirt—looked just as put together as his home. *His neurotic quest for perfection was charming in an odd sort of way,* Brody thought.

"You ready for boys' night out?" Brody asked.

"Hell yeah! Would you like me to get you a drink first?"

"Boy, I trained you well, didn't I?' He smiled. "Don't worry, I'll get it."

"Still in your uniform?"

"Didn't have time to go back to the station. Mind if we stop at my place so I can change?" Brody opened the lid to Myles' ice bucket to find fresh ice and a crystal decanter full of only the best scotch. Next to Myles, this is what he was looking forward to most.

"Sure. I'm good with that." Myles couldn't stop his eyes from raking over Brody's body as he faced away for him pouring his drink. Brody might be his best friend but even Myles could admit he was an incredibly hot guy.

Brody turned back as he took as sip from his glass. Just what he needed. "I waited all day for that." He noticed Myles staring at him intensely, a strange sort of smile on his face. "What are you looking at?"

"Nothing. I rarely see you in uniform. That's all."

Brody was amused at Myles reaction. "I'm guessing you like a man in uniform?"

Myles chuckled. "Who doesn't?"

Brody assumed an unusual cockiness. "So, what do you think?" he asked as he walked towards Myles, an extra bounce in his step and with an exaggerated strut.

Myles laughed uncomfortably. "I think you look less like a real cop and more like a male stripper. No wonder you're able to catch the bad guys so easily."

"A male stripper, huh?" He thought most men would be insulted by the comment. But he was flattered.

Brody removed the handcuffs from his belt. "Have you been a bad boy, Myles?" he said with an over-the-top flirtatious tone.

Myles shrugged. "I may have broken a few laws... now and again."

Brody edged toward him, his moves extremely seductive. "I think someone needs to do a little 'hard time'." He pulled out his iPhone and swiped at the screen. "So I look like a hot stripper to you, huh?" Brody said with a naughty smirk. The room filled with loud thumping music. Then he grabbed Myles forcefully just like he would a suspect and handcuffed him to a kitchen chair. Myles was a bit caught off guard but thought it could be fun to play along and see how far Brody took things.

Both chuckled at the game they were playing. Myles sat as Brody straddled him. Then Brody opened his shirt as his hips thrust and rubbed against Myles, who giggled at Brody's absurdity. The techno music's heavy beat thumped as Brody continued to grind up against Myles' crotch with his ass as the scene became hotter by the second. Brody dropped to his knees, grabbed Myles' belt, and released the clasp. Using his mouth, he slid it out of its loops.

Myles looked down to see Brody looking up at him from his crotch. He could feel his cock getting hard at the thought of Brody opening his pants. He fought the urge to get turned on, but with Brody grinding up against him and opening his pants, there was nothing he could do but feel himself getting hotter and hotter. As Brody continued to grind up against him, Myles could tell that Brody was turned on too. His hands were getting less playful and more seductive with each passing moment. What was happening? When did this turn into a lap dance, and why was Myles feeling so aroused suddenly? Brody shifted to face Myles, his hands resting on the handcuffs fastened to the chair.

Myles felt Brody's breath on his lips. The two men millimeters from each other's faces. In any other world this would be a scene in a bad porn movie. A crazy urge to just lean forward and kiss Brody as hard as he could overcame him. *This is so odd and wrong. Why am I feeling like this about my best friend?*

Suddenly, Brody felt Myles tense up and snapped out of his daze, pulled away quickly, and opened the cuffs. There was an awkwardness that had never before existed between them. Both of them, Brody thought, had been hypnotized, each turned on by the other. This was something new. And Brody wasn't sure how to react and he could tell Myles felt the same. The electric charge between them still crackled in the room.

"We should get going," Myles said, his voice waved.

"Yeah. I'll get my... I'll be in the car."

"Be there in a minute," Myles answered, as he discretely tried to avoid drawing attention to how tight his pants were.

Though the situation was uncomfortable, Brody chuckled at the thought that Myles had to wait a bit for his erection to disappear.

...

Myles waited in the car for Brody to change his clothes. He rarely entered Brody's lair. At thirty-five years of age, Brody still lived like a fraternity boy. Clothes, food, video games everywhere. Myles couldn't imagine living like that, and Brody knew how he felt. So Myles was happy just to wait. Besides, it gave him time to reflect about what had just happened. Was it simply a freak blast of sexual energy between them? *Definitely hot though,* he thought, as he giggled to himself. Before he could think further about what had happened Brody came out wearing civilian clothes and got into the car. Myles glanced at him, wondering what sort of crazy place Brody had picked for the night's adventure.

"So where are we going?" Myles asked.

"You'll see," Brody said as he started the car. Before long they pulled up to a seedy looking bar. Myles thought, *Of course.* As soon as they stepped through the door, they were in the midst of muscular boys gyrating seductively around them. "Really, Brody?" Myles asked. "A go-go bar?" A place where the shirtless, studly bartender obviously knew Brody and what he preferred to drink.

Brody laughed. "Every so often, a guy's gotta get his gay on."

"If you're worried about you not being gay enough, I'd say you're probably good for another year... or ten."

Brody ignored him and turned to the bartender, a handsome man with dark hair and a pearly smile. "Two Goose martini's so dirty the health department will shut your ass down for serving them!"

A Latin muscle god in an Andrew Christian G-string danced on top of the bar. He gyrated over their drinks.

"What is it with you and go-go bars?"

Brody's attention was on the dancer's impossibly large bulge. "What? They've got four of my favorite things here. Hot, almost naked men, booze, and music!"

Myles thought for a moment as he counted in his head, and then gave Brody a confused look.

Brody chuckled and winked. Then Myles understood. Brody had figured him into the equation as the fourth thing. *Shockingly sweet for Brody,* Myles thought.

"You shouldn't snub your nose at go-go bars. They are an important tool in a gay man's sexual arsenal."

Myles couldn't imagine where Brody was going with this but tried to understand. "Like candles and chocolate dipped strawberries?" He tried to solve the riddle on his own but knew that he'd never be able to figure out the way Brody thought.

"What!" He glanced at his friend. "Well, yes and no. Boy, Myles, you need less romance and more sex! Here, follow along. Define go-go boy."

What a ridiculous question! "I don't know. A fit, attractive young man wearing next to nothing, thrusting his engorged...." He gave up. *This is ridiculous,* he thought. "Let's just say a sexy male dancer."

"Exactly! Sexy. Men are visual animals. We see hot guys and get turned on. Go-go boys are eye candy on display to stimulate our adrenaline and increase our testosterone."

Myles still didn't get it.

"These boys are just here to tease. You can't have them. All you can do is look and gently touch." Brody took out a five-dollar bill and waved it in front of the Latin stud. He had the dancer's attention. Was it the five-dollar bill or Brody's bedroom eyes? Not that it mattered. The go-go boy was now along for the ride. He knelt on the bar and leaned back awaiting Brody's next move. Brody took the five-dollar bill and teased the dancer's nipple with it. Both men knew where this was going, and neither seemed to mind. Brody slid the bill over the dancers well-sculpted eight pack and down the front of his perfectly trimmed treasure-trail. Then he stuffed it into the dancer's crotch while gently brushing against his large uncut cock. He turned to Myles. "Yep. No stuffing. It's all man in there."

Under ordinary circumstances Myles would have been jealous of the exchange, but he realized Brody would never be tamed. The dancer had about as much chance of getting anything more than a one-night stand out of Brody than a cheerleader had of scoring a touchdown.

"All this is fine for you Brody, but honestly, what does this have to do with me?" Myles asked.

"Everything, buddy!"

Myles was dying to see how Brody could rationalize this pointless situation. He knew it made sense in Brody's twisted brain, but how could he explain it so it made sense to him?

"Are you saying that guys want them, but the guys will go home with me?"

"That's exactly what I'm saying! You want a man and these boys will help you get one."

"Not for me. I want someone who cares about me. Not someone who has sex with me while fantasizing about some greased-up muscle twink in a G-string."

"Sex is sex, buddy. You've got to lighten up." Myles knew when he's been beaten. This was a dead-end. Brody was never going to be tamed, and he knew it. Sex was sex to Brody and he'd never be able to understand what Myles was looking for. He was running from his feelings, any commitment, and love. Exactly what Myles so desperately wanted. They were on opposite sides of the fence when it came to relationships. If Myles were the "heads" of a coin, Brody would be "tails". That's just the way it was and Myles had no choice to accept it.

"Grab that cutie over there. He's serving mouth shots."

Myles glanced at a cute shirtless twink wearing a G-string and carrying a tray with shot glasses. "And possible meningitis! I'll stick with the cocktail in my partially clean glass," Myles quipped as he looked at the faint lipstick mark on his glass from a previous patron.

Brody sensed that Myles was frustrated at him and their most recent conversation. He had wanted nothing more than to show Myles a good time tonight, but suddenly he could see that Myles was entering into a slump and he needed to act quickly.

"Well, in that case, at least tip the go-go boy. Come on, he likes you. Here!" Brody summoned the same boy as earlier and placed a five-dollar bill in Myles' hand.

"I'd rather not," he said.

"I know, but do it anyway." He motioned for the go-go boy to present his tight ass to Myles, who really didn't mind the taunting. In fact, it was fun. The thought occurred to him that if it weren't for Brody, his life would be all work and no play. Just the opposite of Brody whose life was mostly play and not a lot of work.

"In that case, here you go!" Myles stuffed in the bill like a champ and smacked the go-go boy twice on the ass. He looked at Brody to let him know that everything was fine. He wasn't going to be a downer tonight. He also wanted to prove he wasn't the prude that everyone thought he was.

Brody is obviously taken aback at Myles' skill and assertiveness.

"Hey," Myles told him with a naughty grin, "if I'm going to do it, I might as well do it right!"

CHAPTER FOUR

As Myles sat at his desk in the law firm of Bernstein, Goodman, Scheckman, & Tyler, inundated with paperwork, Diane, his best gal-pal and also an attorney with the firm, walked into his office without so much as a knock on the door. With long brown hair and a slender figure she was smart, cultured, beautiful and classy—the female version of Myles but with Brody's bravado. Like Brody, she was sexually confident and comfortable at expressing her feelings. She sat on the edge of the desk. Obviously, she planned to say something profound and Myles made for the perfect captive audience.

"Please Diane, not now, I'm up to my nose in briefs... And not the good kind." He paused and looked at her with a grin. "If you know what I mean," he said, proud of his Brody-esque pun.

She ignored the protest and bad pun and continued with what she wanted to talk about. "Tell me," she said, "what is wrong with men?"

Myles leaned back in his chair and sighed. When it came to Diane and her needs, there were no other options and it was better to give in and move on. He leaned back, hands behind his head. "At least it's not a complicated question," he said. "Let me clear my calendar for the next decade so we can figure it out."

"Do you have any idea what it's like to have an ovary full of eggs screaming 'fertilize me'? It adds a whole new dimension to the misery of being single."

Myles was getting antsy; he needed to get some work done, and this was certainly not a topic he had time for, nor one he wanted to be dragged into—particularly not at this hour. "No clue, and I prefer not to know. In fact, I don't want to discuss it either."

"Being gay doesn't excuse you from having to deal with this." She stared into his eyes, determined to engage him. He knew he wasn't going to slither out of this conversation – even with the crazy amount of legal work that covered his desk.

"I'm pretty sure it does. Besides, I'm newly single now too." He'd decided that since they were going to have this conversation, he might as well get a little sympathy too and assumed a sad-faced expression.

"That's great!" she said. "It means that next month you and Brody are going to be a couple!"

"What!" He didn't realize he'd told her about the ten-year plan. "When did I tell you about that?"

She gave him a "Bitch, please" look.

He chuckled to himself. There obviously wasn't anything she didn't know about him, and clearly he'd shared more with her about his personal life than he'd originally thought.

"If I know Brody, he's probably forgotten all about it."

She leaned toward him, her eyes piercing. "Then remind him! Brody's a great catch, and he is so damned hot!" She leaned back, message delivered.

Myles was surprised at her reply. Even as boy crazy as she could be, she certainly knew he would never be with Brody. "Diane, he's not relationship material. You know that!"

Diane swung a leg back and forth. "What about you two just fooling around then? I mean, I just don't understand how your best friend is a sexy cop, and you haven't hooked up with him yet!"

Myles couldn't believe she was saying this. "Contrary to what you may think of gay people, we don't all sleep with each other."

"Really? I didn't get that memo and neither did the rest of West Hollywood!"

"Brody is my friend. You don't sleep with your friends."

Diane smiled. "How is it that I never heard of these rules? I swear you make them up as you go along."

"Brody and I don't see each other that way." Diane gave him an incredulous looks as he turned away and picked up some papers, hoping she'd take the hint and let him get some work done. This conversation was getting to personal and cutting a bit close to a nerve. Ordinarily Myles would happily engage Diane in a conversation about how he and Brody were completely wrong for each other, but not today.

"Don't tell me you're not his type!"

Myles laughed sarcastically. This was too easy. He had the perfect retort and he had to use it. "Brody has only one type." Diane knew where he was going with this and followed his lead.

"Facing down!" they said in unison as they laughed at how well they knew each other.

Men always came easily for Diane. Maybe not the right man every time, but there was almost always a man by her side. They would call, and she would answer. What usually followed was one night out and the next one in. No real harm in that if they were both consenting adults. If men could enjoy the fairer sex, then why couldn't the fairer sex enjoy them, as well? Two could play the same game, and what a game it was.

In high school she was always one of the prettiest girls in her class. She was a cheerleader, on the yearbook staff, a member of the debate team, and even the class treasurer. Like Tess McGill in *Working Girl*, she had a head for business and a bod for sin. In spite of all that, she was still her own woman—strong, proud, and determined to make a difference. Law school seemed like a natural choice for her. Northern California born from a prominent family, she wanted to stay in state but still have a chance to get out on her own. The University of San Diego Law School was the perfect fit. It offered warmer, drier weather along with great beaches and a relaxed lifestyle. Diane excelled not only in her studies but socially as well.

In college she dated a number of guys but had one truly serious boyfriend. A teaching assistant, who was a class ahead of her, first introduced Diane to more carnal, if not to say, "kinky," sexual preferences. At first she resisted but slowly he eased her into an appreciation of the less socially discussed forms of intimacy which released feelings and desires in her she had long kept locked away and secret. Their adventures, as he liked to call it, were always a wonderful release and distraction from the pressures of papers and exams. He even proposed to her, but Diane was set on building a career first. She could have her fun along the way as need be, but career was goal number one.

She started at Bernstein, Goodman, Scheckman, & Tyler not long after graduation. Maybe it was her grades that got her the job. Maybe it was her looks. Maybe it was both. Regardless, she was a real lawyer now and she was going to make the most of it.

When Myles first arrived at the firm, Diane was taken with his good looks and friendly, sweet nature. He always dressed well, smelled clean and fresh, and greeted everyone with a warm smile. Myles wasn't like other men who always came on strong. It was a nice change of pace for her to be treated like a person rather than an object to be desired.

She hadn't been dating as much since starting at the firm. The days were long and the weekends even longer sometimes. Thus if a romance developed with Myles, maybe he would understand her schedule better than her more recent, short-term boyfriends.

Whenever she needed to go talk to Myles, she made sure to always look her best. Yet no matter what she did, he never seemed to take the bait. This made Myles all that more appealing to Diane. She craved what she couldn't have. She liked the chase, and this stud was certainly giving it to her. Diane finally made the first move and asked him about having drinks after work one night to further discuss a case. He agreed, and they went to a bar right around the corner from their office.

Talking with Myles was easy. He listened. He paid attention and asked questions. His eyes didn't wander around the bar checking out other women. Myles focused on Diane and took in everything she told him with a sympathetic, reassuring and supportive ear. But when it came to talking about himself, she sensed Myles was a bit more guarded.

He mentioned having gone through a few relationships of late. None were quite working out. He tried too hard, his friend Brody would tell him. Maybe his buddy was right. Myles wanted a relationship too much. He thought Casey was the one for sure this time, but he was scared off too. Diane cocked her head. It was loud in the bar with music playing and everyone trying to talk over everyone else. Did she hear Myles correctly? *He?* She wanted to be sure.

"So what does Casey do for a living, if I may ask?" Diane asked, as she leaned in close for his answer.

"He works for a director's production company reading scripts. No one you've ever heard of."

There it was. That's what he never showed any interest in her. She felt relief mostly but also a little sadness. He seemed like such a catch and she had clearly wasted countless hours fantasizing about what the two of them would be like in bed.

"It's hard to find a good man," Myles said with a melancholy smile.

"Yes, it is," Diane replied. She raised her beer. "To good men."

"To good men," he toasted back. They clinked glasses.

A strikingly good-looking guy, a model type, walked close by their table. For the first time, they both looked away from one another.

They caught each other looking, and then broke out laughing.

"For the record, I saw him first," Myles exclaimed with a smile.

"Not fair. Clearly he was more into me since he passed right next to me," Diane fired back with an equally devilish grin. "Besides you had a boyfriend last, I'm due!"

Myles tilted his head back with a laugh. "Fair enough," he nodded. They toasted again.

Diane knew from here on out that maybe he wasn't boyfriend material, but he was certainly best friend material.

. . .

Myles had another long day at the office trying to clean up everyone else's lives. He loved being a lawyer, but it was exhausting. It was mid-week, and he was already tired. Entering his silent apartment, he flicked on the light. He carefully hung his keys on their designated hook, loosened his tie, and dumped himself onto the couch where he scrolled through his list of phone contacts. Then he shook his head and laid the phone on the table. There was no one he wanted to talk to or see. He'd call Brody, but didn't want to be that co-dependent. They'd seen each other almost every day this past week, and he was sure Brody would enjoy a night off from riding the gloom train with him. Instead, he fixed himself something to eat, not like the elaborate meals he created for various boyfriends, but a plate of leftovers only for himself.

He sighed. What was there to do? Nothing, really. Just another evening alone. Let's face it, he told himself; there was nothing he wanted to do and no one he cared enough to do it with.

He turned on the TV and began to surf the channels. Nothing worth watching, at least that he was in the mood for. He glanced at the clock. How could the second hand move so slowly!

Finally, he grabbed a deck of cards and laid out a game of solitaire. He was bored, totally bored, and feeling sorry for himself. People who said you shouldn't engage in self-pity were wrong. It was good for the soul.

He looked at the clock. It was an hour later, time to go to bed. He peeled off his shirt, revealing his tight swimmer's body, chiseled chest and just the perfect hint of abs under a fine layer of chest hair.

Quickly, he changed from his dress slacks and briefs to a pair of cutoff sweatpants.

Lying back in bed, he began to fantasize. The sexy man who would be his husband. A dark-haired, take-charge kind of guy. Myles would lay his head on the man's broad chest and listen to his heartbeat. He could see himself lying in bed holding the other man, running his fingers through the man's hair as the two of them lay, flesh against flesh. The visual was so real the man almost seemed to be there in the bed beside him. By now Myles had a major hard-on. But there was a problem. He felt too tired to jerk off, but too horny to ignore the large bulge under the sheets.

Then he remembered the toys in the nightstand. What the hell, it wasn't that late. A playful grin crossed his face as he opened the drawer. He reached inside and grabbed the Jeff Stryker dildo, only to find his hand wet and sticky from a jar of spilled lube he couldn't remember buying. *Naturally,* he thought. Why should this be easy?

What a mess! And he couldn't stand messes. He pulled a gym sock from the bottom drawer of the nightstand and began to furiously wipe the soaked toys. Next he pulled out the projector. Damn it! It was sticky too. He placed everything he'd cleaned on the headboard. Then he emptied the drawer of the fleshjack, and wiped it down with another clean sock.

Just then his iPad sprang to life with Brody's grin lighting up the display. Myles couldn't stop the big smile that appeared on his face. Brody was probably just calling wanting to tell him about his latest conquest and Myles felt his smile slip a touch and a too-familiar tinge of jealousy gnaw at him. It happened each time he had to hear about Brody's most recent fuck buddy but Myles chose not to examine that too closely. Though it bothered him, he knew Brody, even with his bachelor lifestyle of reckless abandon, would always be there for him.

He brightened again as he saw Brody's image on the screen when he answered the call. Shirtless and sexy as hell, Myles was sitting alone in a leather chair and eating a burrito with a fork. Brody returned the smile as he saw Myles' image in return on the screen.

Myles liked to think he knew all of Brody's expressions and what they meant, and there was definitely a bit of mischief on his face and he didn't understand why.

"Someone's getting busy tonight! You go, boy!" Brody dropped a bit of burrito onto his chest, picked it up and popped it into his mouth.

Myles was confused. Then he realized: the giant dildo behind his head, the other toys sitting beside it. "Wow." He was embarrassed. "No!"

Brody laughed. "Talk about incriminating evidence!"

Myles tried to dig himself out but only made things worse. "I'm just cleaning up. Everything's covered in lube!"

Brody's smile grew even wider at Myles' words. "Atta boy!"

Myles wished he could shove everything back into the drawer. But it was far too late for that. "It's not what it looks like, Brody." He laughed without humor and shook his head. "But I know you'll never believe me." Maybe if he changed the subject, the teasing would stop. "What do you want, Brody?"

Brody took a final bite of his food. "I'm calling to tell you that someone went south of the border." He raised his eyebrows and grinned. "And I'm not talking about a road trip to Tijuana."

So that was it, Myles thought—the call after the hot hookup!

"I just made it with a crazy hot Latino *papi*. I'm not sure what's gotten into me lately."

It was beneath him, Myles thought, but he couldn't help himself. "Probably about nine inches!"

Brody obviously hadn't been prepared for that sort of answer. He laughed. "Quick. Nice!"

"Well, I was having a nice night by myself," Myles said, his tone sarcastic.

"I could tell!" He was still joking about the sexual paraphernalia lying about on the bed.

"No, no. Not that. I mean I made a terrific dinner—mostly cold leftovers, if you want to know the truth, read a 'good' book—oh yeah, great book, a really, really wonderful book. Then I played some terrific games of solitaire and was about to enjoy a big soft bed without some strange guy next to me, snoring and farting his way through the night."

"You sound miserable." Brody's face filled with sympathy.

Myles wondered if Brody could possibly understand the frustration of having a lot of love to give and no one to share it with. Brody, unlike Myles, spread it around, from bed to bed, whereas Myles endlessly searched for Mr. Right.

"I am."

"Don't worry." Now Brody's face had a look Myles didn't like. Conspiratorial, devious. "I have a plan."

And what could that be? Myles wondered. Then it occurred to him. It may be an opportunity for him to weasel out of the ten-year plan he and Myles had made. Not that he thought either of them would possibly take that seriously. It had occurred to Myles in a flash that Brody had something up his sleeve and he was positive it would be light-years away from his comfort zone. After all, it was indeed ten years next month that they had made their infamous plan to be a couple. Could he be covering his bases and trying to insure Myles wasn't single when their debt came due? Nah, Brody wouldn't do anything that devious… would he?

Myles couldn't help but be suspicious. He knew Brody was up to something. Besides, Brody's plans often weren't the best; in fact, they were often downright disastrous. The go-go bar; the porn shop that at least indirectly contributed to the mess in his nightstand. "And what might that be?"

Brody smiled diabolically. "I'm going to find the perfect man for you."

Myles sat up. "Oh, no."

"Oh, yes." Brody's face now held a new expression, one of determination. "I'm your best friend. Who's more qualified to find someone for you?"

Myles shook his head. "Well, your argument is compelling and, as always, disconcerting."

"Trust me. I've had some great guys over the years. If I weren't a confirmed bachelor, I'd have scooped them up myself. My loss is your gain. I'm going to find you a husband, buddy. You're about to go on a manhunt. So buckle up!"

"I'll brace for impact." Myles warned jokingly as Brody bid him a goodnight and his image disappeared from the iPad as quickly as it came. Myles was once again alone in his bed.

Okay, Myles thought as he lay back against the pillow, *why not give it a try?* After all Brody certainly did know a lot of men—many of whom he said were great guys. Myles frowned. But weren't they Brody's castoffs? No, he chided himself, that wasn't true. Brody was a good guy and his best friend. As Brody said, if he weren't a confirmed bachelor, he'd be living with one of them right now. So why not agree to do as Brody asked? Meet the men his friend would choose for him? Myles was fully aware this could be a disaster. But still, he thought, it was better than being alone.

He fluffed up his pillow, turned off the light on the nightstand and turned over to go to sleep, all prepared now to meet Brody's all-star line-up.

CHAPTER FIVE

In his teens, Myles dreamed of being the next Julia Child. He loved to cook with his mother more than anything else, and it always pleased him when she complimented him on his "unique" or "interesting" meals, in that sweet voice of hers.

"Hey, Myles," his dad often said, "feel like cooking tonight?"

When he looked at his mom after such a request, she usually shrugged. By the age of sixteen he knew he was a better cook than she was. Though he felt guilty about this and pretended it wasn't true, he had decided he wanted to be a professional chef.

As time went on, his mom pretty much relinquished her duties and let him do as he pleased. Whenever possible, he watched cooking channels to find new recipes he wanted to try. But like any good chef, he experimented with them, adding an ingredient to one of the recipes, substituting one ingredient for another. And his sense was unerring... well, most of the time. On those rare occasions when something didn't turn out as well as Myles expected, his dad merely shrugged. "Next time it will be perfect," he told his son.

Myles' specialty was French cuisine. No, his family wasn't French. In fact, their ancestors on both sides came from England. The reason for his style of cooking, he knew, was that he was in love with France—the food, the culture, the language. In fact, French was his favorite subject in school, and he was the top student. But then again he was the top student in every subject.

Unfortunately, his mother put somewhat of a damper on his culinary pursuits in that she told him she hated French cooking. "It's much too saucy," she said. "You'll never get a wife this way." *Or a man,* Myles had thought.

In college, Myles realized maybe there was another way to get to a man's heart, rather than through his stomach. Helping people. So he switched from French language studies to pre-law. He figured he could do some real good in the world and make some nice money while doing it. It was a win/win situation. Myles' father was an attorney, and it afforded them a very nice lifestyle. His dad was an alumnus at USC Law School, so it seemed like the best and most obvious place for Myles to go. Myles was too much of a people person to be locked away in a kitchen and his father was an honest and good man who was popular and helped a great many people out of some very serious situations. It wasn't the creative outlet he desired but it was a sound and logical choice for a good life and career.

After long years of study—college and then law school—Myles was finally receiving his law degree. His parents, who couldn't have been more proud, planned a party for him at a reception hall near the university.

It was a cool and sunny Southern California day, gorgeous weather for the ceremony. As valedictorian, Myles wanted his speech to be beyond reproach, something his classmates would remember for year thereafter. So for months he'd pored over old tomes in the library and spent hours doing research on the Internet. To make sure he did as good a job as possible, Myles even hired an acting coach to help with his delivery. After all, he did live minutes away from Hollywood, which had the world's best coaches.

Of course, the delivery was impeccable, and the content well organized and interesting. He finished to waves of applause. Then came the final part of the ceremony, where the graduates threw their tasseled caps into the air in celebration. But Myles couldn't bring himself to do that. What if he lost it? What if he failed to catch it and it landed in the dirt? He could never stand dirt or disarray. He knew he was more than a little neurotic but just couldn't help himself. In fact, when he was growing up, his mother always bragged to her sister how neat he was—his bed always made, except when he was in it, his dirty clothes immediately placed in the hamper. So at the end, Myles just smiled and kept the cap firmly on his head.

Although his parents were excited about the party, Myles didn't expect many people—his parents and a few aunts, uncles and cousins—to attend. There were two exceptions: his boyfriend, Skye and his roommate, Wayne.

He had met Skye six months earlier and he was everything Myles wasn't—brash, adventurous, easy-going and, to be honest, a bit of slob. But he was a sexy beast and fun. Myles was in love. Well, so was the other guest he expected to attend, his roommate.

Like Myles, he was meticulous, smart, detail-oriented, and loyal to a fault... or so it seemed. Myles and he were good friends and perfect roommates. And much like Myles, Wayne had a super hot boyfriend. But Myles didn't know him very well. He'd only met him once very briefly about six months earlier when he'd come to take Wayne to a concert.

His name was Brody, and he was enrolled in the police academy, hoping to become an L.A. cop. Except for that one time Brody never came to the campus; Wayne and Brody preferred to spend time together away from the dorms. He was a beautiful guy with tussled, dirty blond hair, and piercing hazel eyes. What's more he had a tight muscular body and big kissable lips.

Myles liked Brody immediately; his welcoming and approachable personality easily put him at ease. So, neither objected when Wayne said he'd like to take a photo of his "two best friends." Later, he emailed the photo to Brody.

After the ceremony Myles lost sight of his parents, who, he was sure, had gone to the reception hall. Among the sea of new graduates, their friends, and their families, Myles saw not one familiar face when suddenly he heard his name. He turned to see Brody, warm and smiling.

"Brody, how are you?"

"Ah, you remember me?"

"Of course," Myles answered. Who could forget such a toned, buff Adonis? Well, Myles thought, the day was getting better and better. "Of course I remember you, especially after we posed together, when Wayne took our photo. Besides, he's told me so much about you. You two are a great couple."

Brody wore a tight burgundy tee shirt and perfectly worn and snug jeans, which accentuated his body. Myles was doing his best to avoid cruising him. Committed relationship or not, it's not like Myles was blind.

Suddenly he thought, what if things were the other way around? What if Skye were Wayne's boyfriend and Brody his? He immediately felt terrible. *After all,* he told himself, *I've got the best boyfriend in the world. So what's gotten into me?*

Brody chuckled revealing the cutest dimples Myles had ever seen. "By the way, Wayne thinks you're the greatest—even if you're 'slightly OCD'." He made air quotes that made it obvious those were Wayne's words and not Brody's.

Obsessive Compulsive! Myles thought. Had he just been insulted?

"Thanks... I think. So how can I help you?"

"Oh, sorry. I'm looking for Wayne. I didn't think I was going to be able to make it but I worked it out. I drove up here to surprise him and I wanted to give him this." Brody held up two airline tickets.

"You're planning to kidnap him, are you?" Myles kidded.

"Taking him to Paris." The excitement came off Brody in waves.

"To Paris!" Wow, Myles thought, this guy's too good to be true. Wayne had always bragged about how romantic Brody could be, but this was above and beyond the typical graduation present. Especially from someone still in school. Myles couldn't help himself. "What a gift! You must have saved up for a while to afford it."

"Yup." He grinned, again revealing his dimples. "It's my life savings. I always said that if I proposed, I'd do it in Paris." Suddenly, Brody turned red. "Shit, I wasn't going to tell anyone that!"

"I won't tell," Myles promised. Who was he to ruin such a romantic gesture?

"Please, don't. I'm going to pop the question when we get to the Eiffel tower," Brody said with a smile he couldn't contain.

Myles couldn't be happier with Wayne's good fortune. From what he could tell Brody definitely was a keeper. "How wonderful for both of you. Wayne's a great guy, and he's lucky to have found you. Now let's go look for him. I was just about to try and find my boyfriend too. Let's see if we can spot them in all this mayhem."

Myles and Brody made their way through the crowd. All around them parents hugged their kids; peopled cried tears of joy; congratulations filled the air.

"Great speech by the way," Brody told him.

Myles smiled and felt a little flushed by the compliment. "Thanks. I'm glad you enjoyed it."

"More people should be stopping and telling you how terrific it was. I guess you don't have many friends on campus."

Myles was taken aback. What an odd thing to say. But it was true. No one had stopped to congratulate him, or to mention the speech he'd poured his soul into. How observant Brody was to notice that! Myles thought. He sighed. Maybe he had kept his nose pressed a bit too far into his studies to have made friends. It had never occurred to him before this very moment that with all the students at this university and all the people in his life, he was oddly alone. He was again thankful he had Skye in his life.

Myles looked up ready to respond when he saw something that would stay with him the rest of his life. Brody stood stock-still. Frozen on the spot, his face drained of color. Hazel eyes glassy and wet. *My God,* Myles thought. He followed Brody's gaze across a field behind the campus. At the edge of the field Wayne and Skye were pressed against a tree, locked in a passionate kiss. Myles' heart shattered. It was easy to see this wasn't a first kiss. The two were totally tuned into each other and moved with what could only be familiarity.

It was at that moment, that Brody's heart shut down, the moment he vowed never to be involved again. Never to fall in love. To live his life alone. Myles was hurt too, but clearly not like Brody, who looked as if he wanted to be sick, as if someone had pulled his heart through his chest. He had a look on his face that Myles would never wish on another living soul.

"Listen," Myles told him, through the knot in his own throat, "I don't have any friends here. Actually, really any friends at all, and my parents are having a fancy party for me. I'm about to go there alone and quite honestly, I'd love for you to join me, if you're up to it."

Brody could barely speak as he stared at Wayne and Skye. Finally, he broke his gaze, "Is there an open bar?" he asked.

"Of course."

"Then let's go." Brody said, fighting to keep his eyes from flooding. He and Myles left to attend the party, Brody not saying another word.

CHAPTER SIX

It was a big day. Brody claimed that he had found the "perfect" guy for Myles and had convinced him to date again. He opened his address book and identified his top ten favorite guys of all time. Brody called them and told them that he wanted to set them up with his best bud. Myles had reluctantly agreed to the arrangement but found he was actually a little excited. He was about to meet number one of Brody's exes. *All right,* he thought, as he sat in front of his laptop at the dining room table. *If I'm going to do it,* he told himself, *I'm going to do it right.* And that meant knowing as much as he could about the potential date. He had to make the best of impressions. Yes, he'd researched other men he'd dated, but maybe the problem was he hadn't gone far enough. So he decided he'd learn everything he could about the first man Brody wanted to set him up with. After all, luck was preparation meeting opportunity.

Myles suggested they meet at a fancy restaurant, but Brody advised against it. "Don't overdo it. Keep it casual and easy." He told him to "turn his craziness down from boil to simmer when meeting this guy."

"If you don't like me taking him to dinner at a nice place, what about me cooking for him?" Myles asked.

"He and I met at his house, ordered a pizza and screwed."

"You know that isn't me," Myles answered.

Brody laughed. "Of course, it isn't. Just let me know what you decide."

The first thing Myles discovered was that Stu was a graduate of UCLA, with a major in languages. He had a master's degree in Spanish literature and was now working on his Ph.D. For a couple of years before starting on his doctorate, he'd worked as a Spanish teacher at a private school. This enabled him to save money and rent his own apartment near campus. Well, that was a start. But what did Myles know about Spanish literature? Garcia Lorca and Cervantes—a little bit. That was about it. But okay, he had a week or so to do some brushing up.

The problem of where to meet was solved too. Myles simply looked Stu up on Facebook and found that one of Stu's favorite places to hang out was a particular coffee shop, where he often went to study. Myles did some recon and checked out the place so there would be no surprises. It was a small, mom and pop affair—a much more appropriate date atmosphere than a bustling Starbucks.

It was a homey place where both young and old seemed to gather. The kind of place that reminded Myles of a coffee shop you might have found in a Midwestern town fifty years ago. Or at least that was the idea he had of coffee shops back then and there.

On his solo trip he found the place to be clean and pleasant - it had a nice quiet garden with a fountain in back where you could sit and hear the water trickle. It generally wasn't his kind of place, but he had to admit he had a good feeling meeting there.

In true Myles fashion, he arrived early for the date. The place was nearly full, and he was lucky to find a small table near the front window. He glanced at his phone and saw it was almost time for Stu to arrive. He ordered for himself—and as a result of his research—for Stu, as well. Before long a well-dressed man of about thirty walked into the place, looked around, and approached Myles' table. "Myles?" he asked.

"I am, indeed." He smiled warmly as he indicated the chair opposite him. "It's really nice to meet you. Brody told me a lot about you."

"That's good...I guess." He smiled disarmingly. "I'm Stu, by the way."

"I figured as much," Myles said.

"Sorry." Stu looked embarrassed, and Myles immediately regretted his lame attempt at humor. Being friends with Brody had shifted his filter in ways he'd never expected.

"Don't be; it's okay."

Stu pulled out the chair and sat down. "It's funny you picked this place. It's actually one of my favorite coffee shops... and you ordered me an éclair. I love those."

"Here's a decaf soy latte too." He indicated the cup sitting on the table. "I like to do my research before I meet someone."

Stu had a strange look on his face, a look of disbelief and possibly... concern. "You what?"

"Just a little research, that's all. The more I know about you, the more I can relate to who you are. Just a standard, Google, Facebook, LinkedIn in search was all. I also found some very telling photos of you online. You really need to be careful when posting photos like that. Who knows when an employer may find them. It could get embarrassing." Like this conversation, Myles thought, as he tried to reign himself in.

"I see." He stared at Myles for a moment and then excused himself. "Have to go home and study," he said as he hurried away from the table without even a backward glance.

Had to study! The nerve! Myles thought. He didn't even touch the éclair.

Myles had to admit it, he'd done it again—tried to make everything perfect. But why did everyone object to that? If someone treated him this way, he'd be flattered. Why wasn't Stu? Why weren't any of the others he'd dated? He signed and leaned back in the wire-backed chair.

And so it continued. Before long he felt as if he were on an extra-fast merry-go-round and couldn't jump off, loaded by Brody with a seemingly endless amount of replacement passengers. Only the faces in front of him changed, as did complexions, body types, and hair color. The only things the men had in common were they were in their early thirties and were attractive in their own ways. It became so bad Myles had trouble remembering which date was which, who he had seen, and who Brody had next to introduce him to.

"When you say you like to do your research before you meet someone, what exactly do you mean by that?" Ramón asked. He was a Latino from Belize, with the darkest eyes Myles had ever seen.

"I like to know who I'm meeting. I just like to look at Facebook posts and photos and see if we have any friends in common before I meet them. You know, see if we're compatible. Find out what you're into and who you know."

"So you do this kind of investigation with every guy you go out with?" Cedric asked. He was newly arrived from Britain and was looking for a job in the film industry. Myles gave Brody extra credit for the adorable accent.

"It helps me come up with some things to talk about. There's nothing worse than meeting a guy for the first time and having nothing to say. My research also helps me do things like this..." Myles pulled out a big yellow daisy he'd been holding under the table. "It's your favorite flower. I also know you love to go camping, and you have a French bulldog named Doug."

Jesse's face held a hint of shock. "Would you excuse me?" he said. "I need to use the men's room."

"Want me to order for you? Grande latte with four pumps of vanilla, Right?"

Matt pulled out his phone and glanced at it pretending to look at a text than never actually arrived, and then glanced up at Myles. He was a little younger than the others, from the Pacific Islands. "Oh wow, my sister just swallowed a rusty nail. I'm sorry, I've got to take her to the hospital," he said with a desperate look around the café, obviously looking for the closest exit.

This one didn't even bother with a plausible excuse. *Sister swallowed a rusty nail!* *Yeah, right,* Myles thought. *Just like you got a real text message.* Well, another potential relationship down the drain. He tried to smile. "Call me," he called sarcastically at his retreating form, knowing he'd never hear from this one again either. He thought the only thing to do was laugh at himself, although he didn't feel funny or like laughing at all.

Myles sighed as he sat alone in the coffee shop. Is this really where he was at this point in his romantic life? Was this all real, or was it some sort of nightmare—this carousel of men? Would he wake up in his own bed and find it really was a dream? Well, one thing was sure... he would wake up alone! He was officially finished. This string of dates was the last straw. He knew Brody would blame all these bad dates with great guys on him. He knew that in order for him to be able to defend the last week's worth of coffee-dates and all the effort Brody put into setting him up with all these guys, he'd have to have this conversation in person. Now was the time to break the news to Brody. He was officially done dating, forever.

. . .

Myles pulled up in front of Brody's house. He rang the bell and waited. No answer. But he heard the thumping of attacking zombies and the exploding of grenades. How did he know that sound? It was one of Brody's favorite video games. Here it was, a beautiful Saturday afternoon in Los Angeles, and Brody was shut inside his dark apartment. Myles banged the door again. Still no answer. Out of curiosity, he turned the door handle. It was open. Myles laughed to himself. Well, that was one of the many ways in which they were different. Brody was fearless; Myles wasn't. He couldn't help but laugh at himself for double locking the doors of his home when he's inside, even though he lives in one of the best neighborhoods of West Hollywood He entered the studio apartment to find a shirtless

Brody, face only inches away from the screen. He was playing *Zombie Apocalypse 3* on his video game console.

Myles approached carefully. He felt it was never a good idea to sneak up on a cop. Suddenly, Brody jerked to attention.

"Jesus, Myles! You scared the shit out of me!"

"I tried to let you know I was here; I kept knocking."

"Join me bud, I've got an extra controller here!"

The only videogame Myles had ever played was blackjack on his iPad. He wouldn't begin to know what to do with an Xbox. Besides, he certainly wasn't there to play games. He wanted to let Brody know he was tired of being set up by guys who had no interest in him whatsoever. The type of guys who ran away the first chance they got. These dates did more harm to his ego than good, and he was genuinely defeated, convinced that he'd never find anyone to love.

Brody had a sixth sense about Myles. He knew when he was hurting. He also realized Myles had gone out of the way to have this conversation in person. Even though he knew Myles was upset, he couldn't lead with the concern that he genuinely felt. That was because nothing would needlessly amplify the situation more than feeding into Myles self-pity. It was kind of like when a little kid fell down and you had to pretend like it wasn't a big deal to keep them from going into hysterics.

Brody gave Myles his full attention. "Okay," he kidded, "let's start with mildly melodramatic and work our way back to partially sane."

Myles sighed. "I'm like kryptonite to my Superman. I'll never find someone to love me." Brody thought he may be right. It was sad but true. Myles was a handful. He was like the sun radiating love. Most guys couldn't get anywhere near him without getting third degree burns. Yet Brody was impervious to Myles rays, he thought.

"If I know you, Myles, I'm sure you're coming on a bit too strong. You need to relax, get to know the men you meet. Don't be so serious; have some fun." Brody didn't know if the advice would help or simply make him even more determined to hide in the hermit hole he seemed to want to dig for himself.

Myles perched on the arm of the couch, as usual covered with an accumulation of Brody's belongings. "So it *is* me?"

Brody laid the controller beside him. He'd have to handle this head on. Myles wasn't going to let him dismiss this conversation like he had so many others. "It's not your fault. I've been setting you up with the wrong kind of guy." Brody figured he'd take the bullet for this one.

Myles cocked his head as if to say, *you'd better explain.*

"Give me one more chance, okay?"

"Nope. I'm heading to the kennel, picking out a little white dog, and living the rest of my days alone."

Brody knew Myles was only half-kidding, though obviously he'd resolved not to go on anymore dates.

"This dating thing is just silliness," Myles said. "I can't do it anymore. Honestly I'm done."

Brody turned to face him. "One more date. Promise."

"Absolutely not!" Myles burst out. "No way. I can't do this anymore Brody. No more dating. I've worn my heart on my sleeve for the last fifteen years and it only gets broken–time after time. Please don't ask me to do this."

Brody felt his friend's pain, and he knew dating was hard for Myles. But he couldn't let him give up. Not so much for himself, but for Myles' sake. If you get thrown off a horse, you've got to get back on it. Brody knew that Myles needed a good dating experience to help him heal from this rash of bad ones. He thought for a minute and decided that the best way to insure that Myles went out on a good date was for them to go together. Have a double date. But as usual, Myles was a step ahead of him.

"I have an idea," Myles said. "I'll concede to another date... but only under one condition. And it's non-negotiable."

Brody smiled. "What are your terms, counselor?"

"You come with me. I'm not doing this alone. You pick out a date for me, and I'll pick one out for you." His smile held a hint of irony. "If you're there, then you'll get to witness the disaster first hand. It's like having box seats at a NASCAR race where you know they'll be a multi-car pileup before it's all over. And for once... I won't suffer alone."

It was scary how similarly they thought sometimes even though they were so different.

"Well..." Brody's tone was filled with sarcasm, "as long as you're going into it with such a positive attitude."

"That's right. Positive I'll be alone again at the end of the evening." Both men got exactly what they wanted, a date with a perspective hot guy and to be with each other at the same time. A win/win situation. What could possibly go wrong?

CHAPTER SEVEN

Myles let his date select the restaurant. As chance would have it, it was the very same restaurant that ten years earlier his date ran out on him. The same place where he and Brody made their ten-year plan a decade ago. Myles knew that Brody would never remember that detail, or that they'd even ever been there before but Myles had a head for details and never forgot that date. Despite that, Myles was determined to make a go at having a good time. How bad could it be? He had Brody by his side, and they always had a great time together. And, of course, as always, he'd researched his date.

He found Raul was from Colombia. Myles was ashamed at himself for knowing very little about the country beyond its location in South America. Further research showed it was in the continent's northwest corner bordered by Panama and Venezuela. This wasn't nearly enough. He read up as much as he could, even making extensive notes. Then he researched the man himself.

Now, as he and Brody entered the restaurant, he was sure he'd covered all the bases. It was a high-class place with white tablecloths and waiters wearing black vests and pants and white shirts. Tasteful art, in pastel tones decorated the walls here and there. White candles burned at each table.

Brody spied the table first, near the back, not far from a little stage with a grand piano where a young woman in a sky-blue dress played unobtrusive music.

Their dates had already arrived and were seated, each with a drink... wine for Myles' date and a beer for Brody's. Well, Myles thought, they certainly looked as if they were already enjoying themselves! Upon a second glance he laughed at the fact that Brody and his date were similarly attired in casual shirts and slacks, while Myles' date was meticulously dressed in a blazer and slacks that resembled Myles' own outfit—except Myles was in shades of blue and Raul's in shades of brown. Raul, he realized, was a handsome, dark-haired man with defined features—a very handsome man, in fact.

Myles was impressed by his date's choice in restaurants. He smiled thinking what excellent taste he had by choosing the very same place Myles chose to impress his date a decade earlier.

Myles' date Raul spoke first. "Myles, so good to meet you. I hope you like this place. They have the best stuffed mushrooms." Brody's date quickly interjected. He was a tall sinewy man with brown hair and a serious-looking expression. "I love stuffed mushrooms!"

Myles suddenly tuned out and was lost in thoughts of the last time he'd been to the restaurant. As often happens when a person is deep in thought, the inner dialogue spills out, unintentionally, and Myles found he was talking to himself aloud. "Yeah, I had them the last time I was here. The mushrooms. They were great. It was when my date decided to ditch me." Only then did Myles realize what he'd done and felt completely embarrassed.

The others all had obvious looks of disbelief. Brody rolled his eyes as if to say: Same old Myles. He signaled to Myles to cut it out and just enjoy the sexy man he'd been set up with. A sympathetic look on his face, Raul tried to soften the awkwardness. "I'm sorry about that. Hopefully tonight will be better for you."

He smiled sweetly, but Myles wasn't sure how to diffuse the awkwardness. He raised his glass. "Here's to not being dumped tonight." Myles wasn't sure what to say; he thought that he'd just own his faux pas. Hopefully, everyone would find it cute and amusing. No one was perfect; Myles certainly knew that he wasn't. He thought if nothing else, this could be a test to see how his date handled an awkward situation. Raul unfortunately wasn't prepared for Myles' test. It was obvious he didn't know what to make of him.

He looked toward Brody and shrugged as if to say, "Okay, I'm doing you a favor but now what?"

Brody glanced at Myles and shook his head. "Well, my friend here can be a bit depressing at times. That's why I had the waiter remove all the knives and other sharp objects from the table."

Myles laughed. "You're an asshole." His tone was playful. Brody was trying to save him from this situation, and he very much appreciated it.

Brody's blind date finally spoke up, further adding to the awkwardness of the evening. "You don't recognize me, do you?" The tone was borderline accusatory.

"Should I?" Brody's expression seemed to convey the question: who the hell is this guy anyhow?

"Walter on Grindr? I've tried to chat with you a few times, but you never answer my texts." He leaned forward defiantly, as if to dare Brody to come up with lame excuse.

Brody shrugged like he didn't remember.

Oh, great, Myles thought, it was going to be that kind of evening from beginning to end. How on earth could he have chosen someone who knew Brody, or at least knew about him? Well, that was easy. Brody probably knew most of the men in the whole Southern California area! No, that wasn't fair. He had to admit that part of the problem was his own fault—starting with a negative attitude and spouting off about the last time he'd been here. But this thing with Walter certainly wasn't his fault.

"Sorry, I'm not great with technology," Brody answered, bright-eyed and innocent. "I'm just a simple farm boy." Of course, this wasn't true, Myles knew. Brody was originally from New York City and probably had never even seen a farm in his life except for maybe on TV.

"Oh? Where are you from?" Walter was still on his high horse and obviously didn't believe him.

Brody thought for a second and then shrugged, he didn't care or want to put the effort into manufacturing a lie. "New York."

"Humph!" Walter responded. "And how was the harvest in Manhattan last year?" The question dripped with sarcasm.

"Sorry, Walter, I don't know. I haven't been back home in a couple of years."

"Yeah, sure," Walter answered dismissively.

Well, what else could Myles expect? He had told the guy Brody's name. Why hadn't he simply said he wasn't interested? Because things never worked out, that's why. Why had he ever suggested the double date to begin with? It was something Brody would usually have come up with. Ridiculous.

An awkward silence followed before Raul jumped in to once more try to save the conversation. "I'm originally from Colombia. My parents are farmers. Organic coffee trade."

"There's no such thing as organic coffee," Brody said hoping to fuel a healthy, friendly debate about how ludicrous the price of coffee is and how it's marketed.

"I hear it's just a marketing ploy to drive up the cost of beans," he added in an attempt to help his friend make a point.

Both Raul and Walter were taken aback.

"My family is in the coffee business, too," Walter said. "We sell espresso machines and roasted beans..." He stared at Myles and Brody. "Mostly organic." The last two words meant as a quick jab.

Brody turned to Myles. "A Colombian who grows coffee and an Italian who makes cappuccino? At least they don't fit any stereotypes."

Myles burst out laughing. He wondered if the other two had heard Brody's comment. He decided he didn't care. "Behave," Myles told him, though he secretly enjoyed siding with Brody against their dates.

Raul turned to Walter. "What's your family name?"

"Fiori."

"Yes, I've heard that name. I think my family supplies your coffee beans."

"Get out of here."

The two of them were completely ignoring Myles and Brody—par for the course, Myles thought.

"I'm serious!"

The evening was going nowhere but down. Maybe Myles had been wrong in giving up so easily. He'd give it one more try. "I'm a coffee whore. A double-decaf-latte with soy, extra foam, and extra hot. I don't want to tell you what I'd do for one of those before work."

"And you said it was just a little vanilla froth on the corner of your mouth the other morning," Brody kidded.

"Hey, what goes on between my barista and me is my business," Myles answered.

Brody burst out into laughter, which was infectious. At least for Myles. Not for the other two men, that was certain! Their non-reaction made Myles laugh even harder. Soon he and Brody were giggling like two teenager caught up in the same joke to the exclusion of everyone else in homeroom.

Their laughter borders on the hysterical when they saw the disapproving glances from Raul and Walter. But soon again their dates were wrapped up in their own fondness for each other. Other than the quick look, they turned back to each other ignoring their respective dates.

"Do you know Vincent?" Raul asked Walter.

"Vincent's only my brother!" Walter exclaimed.

Raul shook his head in disbelief. "Crazy small world! What an awesome guy."

"Vincent's been trying to get me to travel with him for years... I think he's even told me about your farm."

"No way," Raul said. "We've got a thousand acres of the lushest farmland you've ever seen..."

Myles and Brody sat in astonishment, watching the magic unfold between their dates. The thing was: Raul was smart, successful...and hot! And sharply dressed besides. Everything Myles had been looking for in a man.

Damn, he thought. What was wrong with him! Wasn't this man exactly the kind worth fighting for instead of giving up so easily? Besides, he and Brody weren't on a date with each other, were they? Of course not. They were best buddies and it was so easy to fall into their usual rapport. And this was supposed to be an opportunity to find a husband, damn it!

Myles decided he wouldn't give up without a last-ditch effort. "So, how about them Dodgers? Looks like it's going to be a rough season coming up, huh?"

Raul obviously didn't recognize the playful nature of Myles' question, but instead his feeble attempt to reset the conversation in his favor and win Raul's attention away from Walter. Raul gave him a direct look, confused and dismissive. "I don't follow sports."

"Sports are something straight guys talk about to each other because they have nothing else interesting to say," Walter interjected, obviously trying to make Myles feel even more ridiculous.

Strike three, Myles thought. Time to throw in the towel. This date, like every other in his recent past, was a bust.

Brody laughed humorously as he spoke only loudly enough for Myles to hear. "I'm starting to regret having the waiter remove those sharp objects."

"Give me a minute, and I'll forge a shiv from a bread stick." Myles figured since this wasn't going anywhere, it was time to have a little fun. Besides, he thought, a night out with his best friend was always a good time, even if it did include stuck-up coffee aficionados.

"Think they'll notice if we leave?" Brody asked.

"I've always wanted to be the guy who leaves," Myles whispered back.

"You know," Brody said, "that's a horrible thing to do to your date."

Myles thought about how many times he'd been ditched and suddenly felt sorry about doing the same thing to Raul. "I know. You're right. We shouldn't do it."

"I didn't say we shouldn't." Brody gave Myles a big smile. "I just said it was horrible. That's what makes it such fun!" He turned to Raul and Walter, with the obvious intention of schooling Myles in how to do it. "Would you excuse me?" he asked politely.

Fun? Myles thought. Well, yes, it was. Fun to be the dumper instead of the dumpee. "I agree," he whispered to Brody. "We need to get of here before I can think any more about it."

"Sure," Raul answered without even looking to see what was going on. He was deep in flirtation mode with Walter, so much so that it seemed to Myles he was trying to close the deal with Brody's date.

"I'm getting up too," Myles said, without Raul or Walter even acknowledging that he'd spoken.

Walter and Raul were perfect for each other, even though they were virtual doppelgangers of Brody and Myles. The difference was that unlike Myles and Brody, Walter and Raul seemed to recognize they'd found their perfect match and were basking in the fact.

Brody and Myles left the table and then turned to look back. Walter was clearing a fallen eyelash from Raul's cheek.

Brody shook his head. "Can you believe this?"

"Oh, I do believe it!" Myles answered. "After all, I have a lot of experience with things like this."

Despite what he'd said to Brody about leaving, Myles began feeling guilty. The sort of behavior he and Brody had engaged in—ditching their dates—was okay for others but not for him. He held himself to higher standards. Admittedly, it felt good to be the one in control, and certainly there was an adrenaline rush to being the one who walks out instead of the guy being jilted, but still, he couldn't help but feel bad that they were walking out on the other two. He shook his head. "I know I shouldn't feel bad about this," he told Brody. "But I do."

"What did I teach you about having feelings?"

"They can only work against you?" he said, echoing the firm sentiment that Brody had permanently etched in his memory.

"Precisely."

As they left the restaurant, Myles figured their dates wouldn't even realize they were gone. It was a clear night, stars twinkling in a cloudless sky. Suddenly, Myles felt better about what they had just done. They climbed into Brody's car. Brody started the motor and turned to Myles. "So the evening isn't a total waste, how about a nightcap at my place?"

"Fine with me," Myles answered, happy that the night wasn't going to end on a down note. Bonus Brody time was never a bad thing.

. . .

When the two men entered Brody's apartment, it was early enough that Myles thought he had a bit more time to spare before calling it an evening. Brody tossed his keys into the tray near the front door. Myles noticed that next to the keys stood the framed photo of the two of them. The identical photo he'd made for himself of the day they first met. Myles smiled. He knew he meant a lot to Brody but for some reason the fact that Brody had displayed the photo of the two of them from that day so prominently made him happy. Brody was oblivious of Myles thoughts; he was on a mission. He grabbed two glasses, dropped in some ice and healthy splashes of Jameson Irish Whiskey and handed one to Myles.

"Well, that went predictably bad." Myles said.

"I'll give you that," Brody answered, resigned to their crash and burn for the evening.

Myles tried to refuse the drink, but Brody put it in his hand anyway.

"I've got a big meeting tomorrow, Brody. Gotta be at my best."

"Jesus, Myles. Just relax for a bit. No need to rush home to Jeff Stryker," he teased. There was no way he was going to let Myles slip out on joining him for a nightcap. Brody loved to toast when having a drink, and he was determined to have a drink with his bestie to finish off the evening. Besides, he thought, it was early, and Myles had nowhere to go. The next day's meeting was just an excuse to get away and brood.

"Who is Jeff Stryker?" Myles asked and then obviously remembered. "Oh, the dildo."

Brody smiled. Myles' naiveté was adorable, he thought. Which was yet another thing Brody loved about him.

Myles noticed a glass with a chicken bone in it on the floor near the couch. He bent down and picked it up. Actually, it was resting in one of the Waterford crystal whiskey glasses Myles had given Brody for Christmas years ago. "You know I can send over my cleaning lady. She's only $75 a visit. She'll even bring her own napalm." He shook his head in obvious disbelief and slight disgust. "You need someone to take care of you."

Brody laughed. Myles was a total neat freak! And he was the opposite. If his place was a little messy, so what? Well, okay, a lot messy—not quite the city dump, but close. "No. I just need to hire a maid." He had no intention in engaging in this line of conversation. This was exactly why he never had Myles come to his home. He knew Myles would have something to say about the way he kept his place, and for Brody, there are just too many other things he'd rather be doing with his time than cleaning.

"Like the old song says," Myles answered, "everyone needs someone, at least sometimes. Even you. What are you afraid of?"

"Being nagged to death about being single. Speaking of... we still need to get you a man!" Myles' criticism reminded him about their ten-year plan and how important it was to find Myles a man before their arrangement became due in just a few weeks. Drastic times demanded drastic measures! He had only one more trick up his sleeve. "Take off your shirt," he told Myles.

If nothing else he'd get him on Grindr where he was sure to meet a lot of hot men. Maybe he'd click with one of them. At least he would be distracted for a bit by how many men were available to him. It was a long shot... but better than nothing. And it was all he had left.

"What?" Myles was alarmed by the sudden request.

"Give me your phone and take off your shirt." Grindr was Brody's way out of this predicament. Why hadn't he thought of it sooner?

Myles frowned. "No way," he fired back. "You're not putting half-naked pictures of me up on 'The Internet'."

"It's not 'The Internet'!" Brody stood facing him. "It's just an app, and everyone does it. Come on; try something new for a change!" Sometimes Myles could be stubborn as hell.

"No." His expression was one of determination. He shook his head. "Tell me, how do you do it?"

Brody couldn't resist a silly answer to an obvious question. "Very well, and often on all fours!" Myles rolled his eyes while Brody laughed at himself. Myles had no idea how easy it really was. And for a guy as handsome as Myles it certainly shouldn't be that hard. Brody felt that this would be the perfect way to keep Myles occupied until their arrangement had clearly come and gone.

"Come on. Trust me. It's better than being alone."

"Well...." It seemed that Myles was staring to yield, at least a little. "I'm really not comfortable with this."

Ah ha, Brody thought, the cause wasn't lost, after all. "Come on, *do it*. Off with the shirt! Show off the goods! It's all advertising." He laughed. "Want to catch a fish? You gotta show them your worm!"

Myles looked aghast. "No one—and I mean no one—is seeing my 'worm', and the shirt's staying on! Non-negotiable."

"Fine. Keep the shirt on." Brody laughed as he demanded Myles give him his phone. Myles complied and Brody took a photo for the profile he was about to make for him. "Say 'I'm a dirty little boy looking for a hot daddy'."

"Cheese," Myles said dryly.

"Cheese will do."

Myles rolled his eyes but then posed for the photo. Brody snapped his picture. *Not ideal,* he thought. It was complete with shirt and awkward smile that somehow Myles still managed to make seem endearing. Not the best bait to catch a man, but it would have to do. He knew it was the only photo he was going to get from Myles tonight.

CHAPTER EIGHT

Brody hit the genetic jackpot when he was born. Hazel eyes, sandy brown hair, a long lean muscular build, and a face to match all his other physical perfections. High school, sports, girls and friends ordinarily come easy to someone with Brody's looks, but none of it really mattered to him.

Brody was born the middle child to the parents of a lower income family originally from New York but had settled in the Valley. His father left his mother when he was young with no child support to care for his younger brother and sister. He was a latchkey kid who knew only one thing: he had to be the man of the family.

When Brody was a child, his father cheated on his mother, and he was the one to shield his brother and sister from his mother's long nights of crying. When Brody's father finally left, it was a welcome relief for the family; however, it meant Brody had to grow up fast. His mother worked in a diner as a waitress. Long, late hours that took their toll. Although she did her best to provide for her family, she was barely able to make ends meet.

High school was especially tough. Brody loved sports but couldn't participate due to his family obligations. He grew to resent the students who had the privilege of being on the teams and took them for granted. He wanted to be on the inside, but he always felt on the outside of what was going on.

Being handsome was a double-edged sword. The attention, the desire, the peer pressure, not only from the girls, who loved him, but also from the guys to be a stud, was unbearable. Brody only ever wanted to be loved, to have a stable family, and to be financially comfortable. All the things he didn't have in his life growing up. He was determined to have them as an adult.

Brody loved people and had tons of friends, but as he grew older, the pressure to have a girlfriend was unbearable. His family and friends were always asking him "How's it going with the ladies?" His buddies always introduced him to girls, who shamelessly flirted with him. Brody wanted to desire the opposite sex, but he didn't. He didn't desire anything. There was something very wrong with him, he thought, but he wasn't able to speak about it to anyone. Besides, who could he talk to? His mother had her problems, and he was essentially the father for his younger brother and older sister. Whatever his problems, he had to deal with them himself.

When Brody turned sixteen, his life changed. He met Wayne at a high school science fair. Brody had finished working out in the high school gym and noticed that something other than sports was going on in the auditorium that day. The large room was buzzing with students from other districts in Los Angeles, which were much wealthier than the one where Brody lived. The students assembled different displays and contraptions. Brody decided to take a look, which is where he first fell in love.

Wayne was in the same grade as Brody but from a rival high school. He was meticulous, organized, sharp, and good-looking in an unconventional way. He was a hot nerd. Something drew Brody to Wayne's area. But it wasn't the display; it was Wayne himself. In fact, after that day Brody couldn't for the life of him even remember what Wayne had entered into the competition. Brody tried to pretend he was interested in the entry, but it was the sexy young man who drew his interest. Brody felt things he'd never felt with a girl.

Wayne was not only handsome, but he was smart, and, unlike everyone else, the only one who seemed to know Brody was gay. The two young men stood talking as Brody did his best to pretend he knew what Wayne was talking about until finally Wayne couldn't take it anymore. The chemistry between them was palpable. Eventually, Wayne asked, "Want to hang out sometime? Maybe come to my part of town?"

Brody didn't know what to make of it at first. Was he asking him out on a date? Was this just an invitation from a guy to just be friends? Brody was confused by the whole thing but knew one thing for sure. He definitely wanted to spend time with Wayne. So his answer was a definite yes.

...

Brody fell quickly for Wayne, a person who was confident and comfortable with who he was. And he'd opened up a whole new world for Brody. Coming out of the closet was never an issue for Wayne because he had never been "in the closet" to begin with. Brody, on the other hand, had had a very different experience. Wayne was not only Brody's first love, but he was the first person of either sex he had ever been with sexually. Brody had tried to make it with girls, but he knew it wouldn't happen. But instead of recognizing what the problem was, he always dismissed them as not being his type.

Wayne encouraged Brody to be his own man on his own terms. They both shared a mutual love for being an underdog, and neither could stand injustice or others being mistreated. They often spoke about how they could help make the world a better place. Wayne had his sights set on law school. He was determined to be an environmental attorney and work for organizations such as Greenpeace or the National Wildlife Defense Fund. Brody didn't have money for college.

He joked that when they eventually got married, Wayne could save the whales and Brody could save the people. Brody knew that with the resources available to him, his best opportunity was to become a police officer. So when Wayne went to college, Brody would go to the academy.

It was Wayne who showed him how different life could be and ultimately, in college, the one who again managed to turn Brody's world upside down.

CHAPTER NINE

Myles lay in bed, naked from the waist up, holding his phone and looking at his goofy photo on Grindr. *No way,* he thought. *I can't go through with this.* It had been a mistake to let Brody talk him into posing for the photo. Well, he didn't have to keep it there, he thought. He could delete it. Brody would be upset, but he'd get over it.

Just as he was about to press delete, there was a chat sound. Okay, he thought, might as well look and see who was sending him a message. What could it hurt?

And there it was: a picture of a very hot man named Hunter. "Wow! Okay then," he said aloud. Maybe Brody's idea wasn't so bad after all. Quickly, Myles typed a response. He wondered what to say, how to be clever. Myles quickly decided on: "Hi. I'm Myles." *Nailed it,* he thought sarcastically.

"Hey, Myles," the man said. "Want to come over?"

An invitation to meet up with just the exchange of a few simple words and a photo? Is he kidding? Myles couldn't believe that such a simple and short exchange could lead to a man like this inviting him over. He didn't even know him! No nerves, no awkwardness, just an invitation he could accept or reject.

How strange and oddly intriguing this was, he thought. Hunter was sexy. No doubt about it. The kind of guy Myles never would consider dating. A rocker with tattoos? How out of the box for him. Now that he had entered Brody's world, he was fascinated. This seemed so alien to him that he couldn't turn away. *How do I know he's not going to kill me?* Myles thought. *A sexy strange man inviting me over in the middle of the night. This could only end badly! Or great...*

Brody had suggested he try Grindr, so it couldn't be that bad, could it? he asked himself. Myles trusted Brody. Although his judgment was questionable from time to time, one thing was certain: Brody would never do anything to put Myles in harm's way. Brody practically lived on Grindr and this was exactly what Myles needed in his life. A break from the ordinary. A little adventure. Something new.

This was really hot, Myles thought, as a thrill surged through his gut. "Come over? You mean right now?" He looked at his watch and weighed his choices.

Brody kept telling him it was this easy, but he'd never believed him. Well, okay, now that he knew he'd give it his best shot. Make up for all the fun he'd lost out on by not listening to his best friend sooner. Hurriedly, he dressed and rushed outside to his car. His fingers actually shook as he tried to insert the key in the ignition. Myles was excited and turned on. This was going to be a night to remember.

...

Myles stood outside Hunter's apartment, terrified. He lived in a red brick building, decades old, with a profusion of flowers blooming in the small space in front. *What was he doing here?* Myles asked himself. Why had he let Brody talk him into something like this? No, he couldn't blame Brody. He had to own this one. He didn't have to pose for the photo. He almost didn't, but he'd given in. And even after Brody snapped the picture, Myles didn't have to let him post it. And, of course, he could have deleted it as soon as he got home. And most of all, he didn't have to respond to Hunter's message or drive across town to see him in the middle of the night.

Here he was, so he might as well see what would happen. He hesitated for a moment and then pushed the bell. The photo hadn't lied because in a minute a hot rocker type, who appeared to be in his early thirties, answered the door.

As usual, Myles had dressed conservatively, while Hunter appeared in a leather vest and wife beater. Was this really happening? Myles thought. It felt like a surreal dream. Myles did not go out with guys like Hunter!

"Cute," Hunter said, his voice a low and sexy timber. "I like the 'Abercrombie meets Log-Cabin-Republican' thing you've got going on."

Myles was a little taken aback. He wasn't sure whether that was a compliment or a criticism. He looked into Hunter's eyes but couldn't read him. No clue there, so he chose to consider it a compliment and stay the course of his new adventure. He took a deep breath. "I just need to tell you that I've never done this kind of thing before."

"And what kind of thing is that?" The other man's tone was slightly teasing.

"Meet up with a guy I don't know in the middle of the night." He was buzzing, a weird combination of excitement and a little terror. A *little?* he asked himself. How could a person be a "little" terrified? You either were or you weren't.

Hunter opened the door a little wider, the tacit invitation there. "And what do you think so far?"

"I'm nervous." About as nervous as he'd ever been, he thought, except maybe when he took the bar exam and then passed with flying colors. First and only time too, unlike many of his classmates. Why in the hell was he thinking of that?

"How adorable."

Again, Hunter was hard to read. Was this sarcasm or a compliment? More like sarcasm, Myles thought. He could still turn around and leave.

"Want to come in?" Direct this time, Hunter stepped back so Myles could enter.

Myles laughed nervously. "You're not going to kill me, are you?"

Hunter smiled. "Do you really think that someone who's planning on killing you is going to answer that question with a yes?"

Myles shook his head. Stupid question, he thought. Obvious answer. The guy looked okay. Not threatening or anything. But this was a big step for Myles. Usually, he met a new man at a restaurant or other neutral spot. Not in the person's home!

"So... feel like taking your chances?"

"I wasn't planning on revealing I was this neurotic until much later," Myles kidded.

"Cat's out of the bag now." Hunter gave Myles the ultimate of sexy smiles and motioned for him to enter. "Offer still stands..."

He stood at the threshold. It was a yes or no move. Enter or leave. Hunter was hot. Just the kind of guy that intrigued Myles. He was everything that Myles had never had before. Maybe this was just the kind of thing he needed. Everything else he'd tried had failed. Drastic times take drastic measures, he told himself. Besides, his bedroom eyes were not something Myles could turn away from. Well, okay. He had come this far, and besides, Hunter seemed sweet enough. *Everyone does this,* he told himself, *and now it's time to have my share of fun.*

"Drink? I've got beer, whiskey, and vodka."

The living room was bathed in light, which reflected off the red walls in an orangish sort of color. It was a retro and funky. Not Myles' choice of décor but not that bad either with red accents here and there—a guitar, a pillow and a candle on a round glass coffee table. Maybe a little overcrowded but neat. Not like Brody's place. The thought made Myles feel disloyal. "Water, please."

Hunter headed for the kitchen as Myles sat in a stuffed chair standing at right angles to a matching, patterned couch. Before Myles had a chance to change his mind about what he was doing Hunter returned with a bottle of water, which he held out to Myles and then sat on the couch. He motioned for Myles to sit beside him.

Myles was hesitant. Was he ready for this? He wasn't at all sure. Oh, what the hell? He sat next to Hunter.

Hunter picked up a bong from the coffee table that Myles had managed to overlook. "Hit?" Hunter asked.

"I'm good." *Drugs?* Myles thought with a quick panic. *I could be a cop!*

Hunter took a hit. "You sure?"

Myles nodded. "So, what happens now?" He glanced around again, as if checking out the best evacuation route.

Hunter shrugged. "Whatever you want." He took off his shirt; a leather necklace and a chain hung from his neck perfectly framing his muscular well-defined pecs. For a rocker, he was certainly well groomed with the perfect amount of trimmed chest hair and a very sexy treasure trail leading down from his navel. He glanced at Myles. "I don't bite... very hard at first."

Myles was clearly turned on and snared in this hot stud's web. He started to panic. What had ever possessed him to do this? He didn't know what was expected. Well, strike that. Of course, he knew what was expected. But he didn't know if he wanted to follow through.

"Sure I can't change your mind about that drink?"

Myles felt quivers in his stomach and took a leap of faith. "Make it a double."

Hunter stood and went to the kitchen. In the meantime Myles decided to give Brody a quick call to tell him what was happening. Maybe Brody could help quell the nervousness and maybe make him a tad jealous in the process.

"What's up?" Brody asked, after just a moment.

Myles hoped Hunter would take at least a couple of minutes to fix the drink, so he could tell Brody what he'd done. He glanced toward the kitchen. So far, so good.

"I took your advice. Check it out." He panned the iPhone's camera around the room.

"Wait, hold it! Where are you?" Brody sounded really concerned.

"Some seriously hot guy's house."

"Don't even say you did it, because I won't believe it." Myles could hear the disbelief in Brody's voice.

He leaned back, a little more relaxed, deciding to enjoy what was happening and to prove to Brody he wasn't the prude his best friend always accused him of being. "This is so hot!"

"Where are you?" It wasn't disbelief in Brody's tone anymore but something that sounded just short of panic.

Well, Myles certainly wasn't going to answer that and have Brody rushing there like the U.S. Cavalry. "His name is Hunter."

"Sure it is."

Myles looked up to see Hunter coming back with two drinks. "Here he comes. I'll call you later!" Myles hung up as Hunter entered with two drinks. Myles hoped he hadn't heard him call Brody.

Myles' phone rang. It was Brody calling back.

"Is that your back up plan?" Myles was afraid he had just insulted him. He knew he had a penchant for always saying the wrong thing at the wrong time to a new guy. Did he just make Hunter think that he's not into him and trying to set up someone else for the evening?

"What? Huh. No it's my buddy. He always calls me when he meets a hot guy, and I just called him." Myles blurted out the truth to try to save him from the awkwardness of the situation.

"I'm flattered."

The phone continued to ring.

"Sorry."

"Get it, if you want," Hunter said as he lounged once more on the couch toying with his necklaces.

"Just one second." Myles stood and stepped away so Hunter wouldn't hear. He was just the least bit irritated, though he knew Brody had his best interest at heart. "What's up?"

"What are you doing?"

Really! Myles thought. Was this necessary? "I'm taking your advice."

"*My* advice?"

"Meet people. Have fun. *Post my picture on Grindr!* I gotta go. I don't want to be rude. Call you later."

"No, wait!"

"Call you later!"

"Make sure you call me!"

Myles hung up and went back to the couch. He couldn't continue this nonsense. Brody could ruin what promised to be a very hot night with a mysterious stranger. Myles was warming up to the evening and starting to enjoy where this was going. Mostly because he knew that now Brody was home going insane about what he was about to do and who he was about to do it with. "That was ridiculous, wasn't it? Now I'm embarrassed." And he was. He had to admit that yes, he appreciated Brody's concern, but he also resented his call. After all Myles *was* a fully responsible adult.

"No. Don't be, it's sweet."

Again, Myles didn't know how to read Hunter. Did he mean what he said or was his tone a little off?

"Well," Hunter continued, "if there's no one else you'd like to ring up at midnight, are you ready to get to know each other better?" Hunter reached over and put his hand on Myles' leg.

Myles pulled back. Damn, why did he do that? Hunter was sure to think he was a total neurotic—a Woody Allen type, for heaven's sake. Still... who puts his hand on another guy's thigh after meeting him only five minutes earlier? Hunter's intention was clear. Obviously, he wanted to see Myles' reaction. Myles knew that if he gave him a consensual smile, Hunter would slide his hand right up to his crotch! Myles reeled from the surprise that Hunter was ready to start the evening with a casual fuck.

Myles simply couldn't grasp the idea of no conversation first; no discussion on what each of them liked and was into. Hunter didn't even know him and he was happy to jump into bed!

"Mind if we just hang out tonight?" Myles needed time to process what was going on. But oh, man, he was tempted. What was wrong with him? He'd known what to expect in replying to Hunter on Grindr. So why was he turning into a virgin, all at once? He certainly wasn't one. A virgin, that is. Myles took a deep breath and regrouped.

"Oh. Okay. No worries. I'm fine with whatever."

Could Hunter really mean that? It certainly wasn't the evening Hunter had expected, now was it?

Myles asked him. "You sure?"

"Yeah. I just assumed that's what you wanted."

"I'm not really like that." What a stupid thing to say, Myles told himself. Not like what? No, he was far from a virgin... but Hunter probably wouldn't believe that. And by saying what he had, wasn't he implying that he was somehow better than Hunter? Leave it to me, he thought. Able to handle any situation that might arise. Uh huh, sure!

"Me neither," Hunter answered a little coyly. "I'm actually really just a simple romantic homebody. I'm good with just hanging out tonight."

Myles relaxed. Maybe things weren't so bad after all. "That's very cool of you. You seem like a really great guy."

"I do."

There was an awkward silence. Then suddenly Myles changed his mind. He had obviously misjudged Hunter. He was probably just as nervous and awkward as Myles. Besides, Hunter had just admitted to being a "simple romantic-homebody". That meant the two men had more in common than Myles had originally thought. Myles felt bad that he had been so quick to judge Hunter. The rock and roll persona was probably just a way to protect the sweet romantic he was inside.

People had often misjudged Myles as being a shark just because he was an attorney. He was now doing the same to Hunter. Clearly he had met a sweet man just like himself, who was just looking for a connection. Someone to love, just like Myles was. "You know... it's okay if you want to put your hand on my leg. I won't freak out on you. Promise."

They stared at each other for a moment, and then Hunter placed his hand on Myles' upper thigh. It sat there for a moment. The physical contact felt good, and Myles couldn't deny that Hunter turned him on. Myles nodded. Hunter again reached out further running his hand up his leg until he had it on Myles' crotch, then gently squeezed Myles' cock, which clearly indicated his approval of what was going on. He waited for Myles' reaction.

Myles suddenly sprang into action. He grabbed Hunter and threw him backwards on the couch. Like a rag doll, Myles thought, before he climbed on top and kissed him—wildly, passionately.

Myles had been repressed too long. Always playing the role of the perfect husband; conservative to a fault, so as not scare away the perfect man. Tonight was long overdue. This sexy rocker was just what Myles needed, and the encounter unleashed something Myles didn't even know was inside him—a propensity for rough, anonymous man-on-man sex without judgment or boundaries. It was if he'd lost total control, and Hunter was the lucky recipient of all Myles' years of pent-up his passion.

Fortunately, Hunter was up for the task!

"Oh, man, you really were ready, weren't you!" Hunter said. They pressed against each other hard, lips pressed tightly together. After a time both stood and stripped down. Myles' shirt was the first to be peeled off, revealing his sweat-covered chest and defined abs.

Myles was only slightly aware of the rock paraphernalia that filled the room, the darkly painted walls, and three or four guitars in corners. He had the fleeting thought that Hunter's apartment was like a fan-ravished Van Halen tour bus. Somehow it added to encounter.

Quickly, Myles mounted the other man, and then they switched. Hunter held Myles' hands down as he had his way with him. Myles decided to try new tricks, to allow himself to be uninhibited. And he followed through, over and over again. An hour later, Hunter told Myles he was exhausted, and the fun had to end.

Myles wasn't sure how he felt about that. Something had been released inside him and reminded him of a feral animal in heat.

"Oh no." Myles shook his head. He grasped Hunter's hand. "Which way to the bedroom?" There was no sleep for either of them till the early hour of the morning.

CHAPTER TEN

The next day Brody and Richard were in the police station locker room changing into their uniforms. "I'm worried about Myles," he told Richard.

"How so?"

Extremely upset, he tried to explain. "Myles met this guy last night."

"Great! Isn't that what you wanted?"

"Well, yes, but—" He couldn't put to words why this was a bad thing. It just wasn't Myles.

Just then Brody's phone rang. He saw the number was Myles' office. "What the hell happened to you last night?" He was angry and concerned. "You never called me back!"

"It's Diane." The feminine voice momentarily halted his tirade. "Do you know where Myles is? It's ten thirty!"

Brody was surprised and distressed by this. He's not at work? Myles would never be late for work. Something must have happened! Myles could be so damned naïve, taking everyone at face value. But that wasn't the way the world worked; there were a lot of nasty people out there. As a cop, Brody was more attuned to the facts and certainly more able to handle himself in a dangerous situation. *Something must have happened to him,* he thought. His police academy training kicked in and Brody went into crisis mode.

Without thinking Brody blurted out the obvious. "He should be at the office."

"Oh." Her tone was sarcastic. "Maybe he's here after all. I forgot to look around. Hold on, let me check the other three corners of his office. *No, he's not here!"*

He didn't appreciate the sarcasm, but considering the situation, he pushed his resentment aside. Besides, she sounded as worried as he was. "Did you try him at home?"

"It's a wonder you're not a detective yet." By now her voice dripped with mockery.

He decided to ignore her tone and press on. He was more concerned about his friend than about correcting Diane on how to be socially tactful. "I haven't talked to him since last night." He began to panic.

"He had a client meeting on his books at ten, and he missed it."

"I'll go by his place to check on him. Give me ten minutes. I'll get back to you." Brody was clearly shaken by the fact that Myles was now MIA. They changed quickly into their uniforms and headed out to investigate what was happening with Myles.

. . .

Myles was still asleep in Hunter's bed, snuggled beneath a patchwork quilt. Hunter woke him with a cup of coffee. At first Myles was confused. Where they hell was he, and what was going on? Suddenly, he remembered. Grindr. Coming to a strange person's house. A night of wild sex. Oh, yes. Hunter. Already, he was half in love! Well, not really, but he certainly could be, given a little more time with him.

Hunter presented the hot coffee to Myles.

"Aw, how sweet." Myles said, sitting up and taking the cup. What a wonderfully thoughtful way to greet your partner in bed? This one may be a keeper, he thought.

He was getting dressed as Myles lay in bed. He pulled his shirt over his head as he stood there in his gym shorts. "Well, that was certainly hot."

Myles smiled at him. "I needed that."

"Apparently several times." He laughed politely trying to give Myles a not so subtle hint that it was time for Myles to leave. "Listen, I have to go. I've got class."

"Oh. What are you studying?" Myles asked with no intention of doing anything other than enjoying the hot coffee and getting to know this stud better.

"It's an aerobics class." A feeble attempt to be adorable.

"Ah. Is it tough?" He was kidding but the tone held a hint of teasing.

Hunter's answer was defensive and a bit dismissive. "It's actually quite fun."

"No. I mean getting back to the 1980's – back when they actually taught aerobics." Myles chuckled at his own acerbic wit. Hunter was stone-faced.

"It's coming back, I'll have you know."

"I'll have to remember to tell my leg warmers." Again, he was kidding but could tell Hunter was far from amused. What made him say things like that, he wondered? A nice man. Relationship potential, to say the least. And here he was, letting his stupid sense of humor control him.

"What are leg warmers?" Hunter asked with a slight curiosity still hoping that Myles would get the hint that he's dressed to leave and edging towards the door?

"You're kidding, right?" Did he really not know what leg warmers were?

"No, and unfortunately I don't have time to find out. I need to leave. I've got to be there at eleven."

"Eleven!" For the first time Myles spied a clock on the wall. "Oh, my God."

Myles realized what was going on finally and remembered his morning meetings. He grabbed his clothes from off the chair and quickly got dressed. He'd call Diane in the car and tell her was on his way.

...

Brody knocked on the door to Myles' apartment. "Open up. Are you in there?" He'd never forgive himself if anything happened to Myles. What had ever possessed him to talk him into posting his picture on Grindr?

"Don't you have a key?" Richard asked.

"Why would I need one?" He pulled out a lock-picking kit. Across the hall, a door opened and Mr. Harrington, an older man stuck his head out. He looked to be about sixty with a white beard, brown hair, and a solid build.

"Is there a problem, officers?" Mr. Harrington asked.

"No," Brody answered as he hid the lock picking kit away from sight. "We're just responding to a call. Do you know Myles?"

"I do. Quiet fella, but nice. Always a hello in the hallway. Raised right. Smells good too." He paused, the typical nosey neighbor. "What did he do?" His tone was filled with suspicion.

For heaven's sakes, Brody thought. So he's that kind of neighbor. Wanting the latest gossip. "He didn't do anything. We're just checking on him. Did you happen to see him last night?"

"Nope. Don't think he came home, or I would've heard him. I hear everything. Even with this bad ear." He pointed to one of his ears. "I catch it all." He paused. "Let me know if you need my help. I'm a vigilante, you know."

A vigilante. Oh, sure he was. This was exactly the kind of old coot that called in every complaint imaginable to the station. Just what Brody needed to start a bad day. "I've got it covered. Thank you for your help," Brody responded as politely as he could muster.

"Anything for officers of the law." The guy was a brownnoser too. "Keep up the good work, boys." The neighbor disappeared back into his apartment content that the two officers were doing their job.

Brody shook his head in disbelief before using his kit to open the door. In just a few seconds he and Richard walked inside.

"Myles? Myles?" Brody called and then looked around. He looked inside the bathroom. Nothing. The bedroom. No one. And the kitchen. Not there either. Oh, my God, what had Brody done? Myles couldn't handle himself in a bad situation. He didn't have the training, the know how. Brody was starting to get upset, so upset he could hardly concentrate on what he was doing.

"Wow. Who's his roommate, Mr. Clean?" Richard looked at the bar admiringly. "A carafe? Silver shaker?" He picked up the latter to look more closely. "Who does he entertain here? James Bond?" He shook his head in disbelief. "So," he said, glancing at a stack of DVDs, "when Blockbuster runs out of movies rent to their customers, do they come here and borrow a few from Myles?"

Richard was doing his best to lighten the mood. He desperately wanted to diffuse Brody's angst. He knew that Myles was a smart man who could handle himself and wasn't in the least bit worried. Brody, however, was on the edge of his last nerve.

"Enough with the commentary! Just see if you can find anything." Brody barked at him as he continued to look through the apartment—in closet doors and everywhere else he could think of. Where in the hell was he? What was going on? This wasn't at all like Myles. He was the epitome of responsibility.

"Like dust? Good luck with that."

And why wasn't Richard more concerned! Brody didn't understand. Suddenly, he noticed a suit hanging over the bedroom door. "Oh, man, that's what he was planning to wear today. That means he never came home last night." He was breathing hard. *Where are you, Myles! Where are you?* he thought. This was all his fault! Brody didn't even know where he'd gone. It could be anywhere in the city.

"I'm sure he's fine," Richard said.

"Famous last words just before we find the body in a dumpster. We've got to put out an APB. Get more eyes out there looking for him."

Richard had never seen this side of Brody before, his genuine concern for someone. He knew Myles meant the world to him, but Brody's voice held sheer panic, as if to ask, "What if something happened to him?"

Richard decided instead of trying to make light of the situation, he'd change his tactics. Brody needed support right now, not humor.

"Before we sound the alarm, let's stop by his office and see what we can find there." There was a look of sympathy on Richard's face. "Relax. It'll be fine. One quick stop. Okay?"

Richard corralled Brody out of the apartment and back out onto the street.

. . .

Back in Myles office, Diane's cell phone rang. She reached into her pocket, pulled it out, and answered. It was Myles. "I've been calling you," he said. "You're not answering your office phone."

Whew! It seemed he was okay, she thought. "I'm in *your* office. Where are you?" Now she was annoyed. Where had he been anyhow? What had he been thinking, scaring everyone half to death? "You had a 10 o'clock client!"

Why was she so concerned, for heaven's sake? It wasn't like he'd been missing for days. "I overslept."

Sure you did, she thought. "I know you better than that. What's going on, Myles?"

"Nothing. It's all good." He paused for a moment. "What happened with my client?"

"I covered for you. Everything's been handled, but you need to call Brody. He's about to drag the river looking for your body."

"You called Brody?" Why would she do that?! And why hadn't he called Brody like he promised? Well, that was easy enough to answer. He grinned to himself. He'd just been a little bit too busy.

"You had me worried. You're never late or miss work. What was I supposed to do?"

"That's not true, Diane." But it was true, he thought. Old dependable Myles. Old predictable Myles. Well, not so predictable now, was he! "Please! You make Old Faithful look like a slacker, and Big Ben calls you to find out the time."

"Well, I'm here now. I'm just walking in..." Myles entered still on the phone. When he saw Diane, he hung up. He gave her a smile. "Thanks for covering for me."

She looked at him, clearly puzzled. "Just hold it, Myles. Why are you dressed like that? Is this a walk of shame?"

Of course, he wore the same "Abercrombie" clothes he'd had on when he'd gone to Hunter's house—a knit shirt and slacks rather than his usual lawyerly suit.

"I'm not ashamed of anything."

"Then you obviously didn't do it right," she answered back with a smirk.

Myles grinned. "I wouldn't be so sure about that."

She sat on the edge of his desk. "Okay, tell me what happened. And it better be filthy. Pictures, descriptions, names, and phone numbers. Is video asking too much?" She smiled in anticipation.

Diane loved details and she loved Myles. This was something she'd clear her calendar for. She wanted to know everything about Myles' tryst. He had clearly gone out of his comfort zone and done something unexpected and naughty. She was proud of him and dying for the details.

"A gentleman doesn't kiss and tell." Myles sat at his desk and leafed through some papers, obviously trying to indicate to her that he was busy and didn't want to discuss what happened, at least at the moment. She knew that inside he was probably dying to tell her about his night. He did have a ton of work, but nevertheless…

"A gentleman who doesn't tell is asking for a beating," she threatened.

"Fine, but only because you scare me…"

Diane picked up her phone. "Wait. Hold that thought for one second. Before you start, let me call Brody so he can call off the SWAT team he's about to send looking for you." Diane dialed, and they heard a ringing sound from the hallway.

In a moment Brody and Richard walked into the office as if they were about to seize the building and conduct a full manhunt for the missing Myles.

"I was just calling you…" Diane said as she put down the phone.

"See?" Richard said. "I told you he was fine."

Brody turned to Diane, "Has he been here the whole time?"

Brody was thrilled to see his friend; it felt like a thousand pounds had been lifted off his chest and he could breathe better than he had in an hour. But he wasn't going to let Myles know he been afraid something bad had happened to him. The wall would stay up till he received some answers.

"He just showed up. Hence, I just called you." Diane's tone was a little confrontational.

"Hello," Myles said, "I'm standing right here. You can address me directly."

"Diane said you didn't come to work today. She had us all worried."

"I just came in a little late." He looked toward Diane. "You really didn't need to call Brody."

"Don't blame me. It's my maternal instincts. I'm a hostage to them." Suddenly, she became aware of Richard standing by Brody.

As they all knew, Diane liked Latin men, and it was easy to see this big Mexican stud was exactly what she wanted. In fact, if the situation were different, Brody might have laughed at her oh, so obvious, attempts to attract his full attention

"Hold it," Diane said. "All at once it seems this whole series of events has made a turn for the better." She held out her hand, palm down. "Hello. I'm Diane. I hope you enjoy the softer of the two sexes."

Richard kissed the back of the outstretched hand. "Hi. I'm Officer Garcia... and I do." Richard was equally happy to make Diane's acquaintance.

Brody was still upset, especially now that no one else seemed to be. "Where were you? I thought something happened to you!" He scolded Myles like a child.

"Something did." Myles smiled broadly.

Diana turned back to Brody. "He was just about to tell me. I'm dying to hear the sordid details. I have a feeling that most of them are filthy."

"It'll have to wait. I've got work to catch up on this morning," Myles said. "Now if you'd excuse me." All this reaction over nothing! So he was a little late to work and had so much to do. This was clearly going to turn into something more than he wanted it to.

They were all standing in the middle of his law office. Other lawyers and paralegals were starting to look and listen. All Myles needed now was for one of the firm's partners to walk by and see him sharing the sordid details of a sex date with Diane and two cops. He had to postpone this de-briefing until later, at a time and place when the conversation would be more appropriate.

"Is he kidding?" Brody asked.

"Give me a minute."

"Take all the time you need." Diana addressed Richard. "And you. Come with me." She stepped out of the office, and Richard followed. Myles realized Diane was about to spin her web, and Richard was the fly caught in it, not that he seemed to mind. Diane cozied up to a filing cabinet just outside Myles' office and took her most seductive pose.

"Okay, what happened last night?" Brody demanded. He was curious as to what was going on in Myles' head and how he could be so inconsiderate of his best friend's feelings. "And what were you thinking going to a stranger's house in the middle of the night for a hook up?"

"It was your idea. I'm trying new things. Plus, you do it all the time."

"I'm different."

"How so?" Brody could tell Myles was becoming irritated.

"I'm a cop. I can take care of myself. You on the other hand..."

"Oh, please." This had gone far enough, Myles thought. He didn't have to put up with any more of it. Why was Brody behaving like this? He was a grown man and could do whatever he wanted. Besides, it was all Brody's idea. How dare he give Myles such grief? If Myles had committed a crime by doing what he did last night, surely Brody had multiple violations of the same crime on his record!

"I know guys who are real creeps. I see what people are capable of!"

"I appreciate your concern. Really, I do. But I can take care of myself, thank you." Myles could see Brody was shaken by his disappearance. Did Brody genuinely care that something could have happened to Myles? Could he be this upset by his brief absence? Myles knew Brody cared about him, but not to such an extent. Myles suddenly realized that Brody's anger was coming purely from a place of caring and concern. Myles' part-annoyance quickly turned into a sweeter sentiment. He realized that Brody was afraid for the first time in a very long time that someone he cared about could have been in trouble. With that Myles gave Brody a warm smile.

At first Brody seemed to be taken aback, unsure what to make of Myles ridiculous grin.

Then each of them seemed to realize the jig was up and that Brody had been overreacting to Myles being missing because he really cared. Brody suddenly seemed to give in and approach the situation with humor. "Like you did that time when those girl scouts muscled you into buying a dozen boxes of cookies." Brody broke out laughing.

"That wasn't my fault." Myles mock protested, the tension broken. "There were four of them and only one of me."

"So, do you have a first name, *Officer* Garcia?" Diane asked as they leaned against an oversized file cabinet.

"It's Richard."

She grinned wickedly. "As in...?" Her eyes devoured his body and she tried to lead him down a very flirtatious path.

"Yes. Richard." He clearly hadn't picked up on the sexual innuendo.

Diane looked him over. She certainly wasn't going to relent and give up on a man this hot. She wanted him, and badly. Moreover, she was going to get him. "Uh, huh. And you're packing a lot of equipment there." As she not so subtly looked down at his crotch.

Richard finally realized she wasn't talking about his nightstick and gun. "We're outfitted with the proper gear to handle any situation."

Well, good, she thought. Playing dumb was only a pretense. She flirted her way and he responded his way. *The attraction seems to be mutual,* Diane thought. She hoped he wanted her as much as she wanted him. If so, why was he playing at being so hard to get? As the king of Siam used to say to his audiences each night, it was a puzzlement.

"I can see that." All at once she was Mae West. "So what's a girl gotta do to get her hands on your nightstick?" The playing continued. Myles and Brody on the other hand were done with their argument. Both resolved in what had happened and they were in agreement that they both needed to get on with their day.

"Look, I've got to get back to the station. Can we argue about this later?"

"Maybe, if I'm not too busy, *Dad.*" Myles said to drive his last point home. Brody shook his head and left the office to gather Richard and head back to their beat.

Diane shot Myles a quick look through the office door. She mouthed the words, "OH MY GOD" to Myles. She was clearly smitten. Myles knew she was a woman on a mission and her target was Richard.

CHAPTER ELEVEN

"So what's with Diane?" Richard asked as they slipped into their police cruiser. Richard was wasting no time in getting the "411" about Diane.

"I know. I'm sorry you got stuck with her. She's insane." Brody rolled his eyes as he raised the volume on the dispatch radio.

"I felt like a piece of raw meat for her to chew on and spit out." Richard gave Brody a big grin. "How awesome is that?"

"Wait. What?" Brody couldn't hide his surprise. Richard and Diane? Nah, it would never work.

"*Muy caliente.*" The devilish grin and wagging eyebrows looked almost out of place on Richard's usually more serious face.

"Diane? As in... you and Diane? No. Bad idea. You two couldn't be more different." Diane and his partner? He couldn't believe it.

"Friction is what makes the heat, my friend. Besides, I'm packing... and I also carry a gun."

"Let's leave the bad sexual puns to me," Brody said but he was pleased that his partner was finally developing a sense of humor after years of being very literal in his approach to life.

Richard turned serious. "So, what happened with Myles last night?" he asked Brody. "How and why had he seemed to have disappeared off the face of the earth?"

"He met some guy on Grindr and stayed with him all night. It was apparently a very active night. He said he didn't wake up till almost eleven. I didn't ask for the details but if I know Myles, he's already smitten."

"That's great. Your plan worked."

"I guess it did, right?" He should feel good about that, he thought; instead, he felt something he couldn't quite place. Discouraged? But why? Things were working out in his favor.

"You should be happy. Looks like you're off the hook. Beers on me tonight. You pick the place."

He should be thrilled, Brody thought, but he wasn't and didn't know why. What a day he'd had so far. It was over now and nothing more to think about. Tonight drinks were on Richard. That was good enough for him.

Richard told Brody that he could pick the place. Of course, he picked his favorite dive bar complete with go-go boys and hot men. *Why not?* Brody thought. He'd been to his share of straight bars with Richard. It was only fitting that Richard come with him to his favorite. It was loud, as usual, and filled to capacity.

He and Richard now sat at the bar with drinks in front of them. Suddenly, a crotch gyrated in Richard's face. It was Brody's favorite go-go boy. Brody had tipped him heavily in the past, so this buff young dancer tried to coax a few tips out of Brody's friend, obviously thinking he'd tip well too.

Richard leaned over toward Brody. "He clearly doesn't know I carry a gun."

"He likes you." Brody took a five-dollar bill from his wallet and jammed it into the front of the dancer's skimpy shorts to appease the dancer.

"Great. Now he's going to like me that much more!"

"Hey, I've gone to enough titty bars. You can get your go-go on with me."

"In that case, I need another drink!" Richard waved over to one of the shot boys and held out a bill. It was a shot boy who was working the room selling "mouth shots". He picked up the bottle from the tray he carried and drank from it. Then he grabbed Richard by the head and spits the alcohol into his mouth.

Richard jumped off of the barstool and spat furiously. He rubbed his mouth hard with the back of his hand trying to wipe off the germs from the shirtless twink's mouth. Brody had never seen him move so quickly and he'd seen him take down armed perps in the past.

The bar was suddenly quiet, everyone staring.

"What the hell are you doing?" Richard was angry. He seized the boy's arm as everyone else looked on astounded. Suddenly, Richard realized where he was and how he was reacting. The kid was only doing his job, and the tray he carried did advertise "Mouth shots for five dollars".

"I'm sorry. You just caught me off guard," Richard apologized, realizing he appeared not only homophobic but like a bully, as well.

The tension in the bar suddenly disappeared as the boy scampered away. Richard turned and gave Brody a dirty look.

"I was going to warn you about that." Brody laughed

He rolled his eyes. "No, you weren't."

"They're called mouth shots for a reason," Brody explained, realizing that Richard could never know that since it wasn't something that ever occurred in a straight bar.

"What the hell other kind of shots are there?"

Brody stared at him as if to say, "I can elaborate on the subject if you'd care for me to."

"Okay, I really don't want to know," Richard said as he checked his watch. "All right," he told Brody. "I gotta run."

"Where are you going?"

"I told Diane we could meet later. After she got off work."

One quick drink and Richard was planning on leaving? That was bad enough. Brody was looking forward to drinking with his partner tonight. But to leave him to meet up with Diane? *Oh, no,* Brody thought. Diane was fun and cool but definitely not Richard's type. He hadn't thought about what Richard's type was before this very instant, but Diane? Definitely not.

Richard was the greatest guy with the biggest heart. Diane was a sassy, wisecracking, sex-crazed powerhouse. The two were compete opposites, totally incompatible. Like he and Myles were. Brody knew that Richard would have to learn the hard way that he and Diane were a bad idea.

"You're just going to leave me here alone?" Brody asked.

"You're not alone. You have your friend here to keep you company." Richard was referring to the go-go dancer in front of him. Richard pulled a twenty dollar bill out of his wallet and waved it in front of the dancer. He obviously had chosen not to stuff it in his thong. Richard smiled to himself before handing the money to Brody to stuff it in the dancer's thong for him.

Richard told the dancer, "This is so you'll pay a little extra attention to my friend." He indicated Brody.

The dancer plucked the money from Richard's hand, and with a wink let Richard know he'd make good on the exchange. Richard patted his partner on the back and headed out of the bar on his way to Diane's.

CHAPTER TWELVE

Richard couldn't stop thinking about Diane. She was aggressive, smart, and gorgeous but best of all, she not only talked the talk but also most certainly walked the walk.

He arrived at her house ten minutes early. It'd been nearly eight months since he had been on a formal date with anyone, and he wanted to be on time and make a good impression. Richard sat in the car outside of her house, looking at his watch impatiently. Then he examined himself in the rearview mirror. After turning this way and that, and looking himself over, he decided he'd waited long enough. Hopefully she'd not mind his arriving a bit early. Richard looked at his watch one last time, climbed from the car, and headed to her front door.

Her smiled dazzled him. It was so bright, he thought, it could melt polar ice caps. She wore a clinging red dress with a low neckline. *Beautiful,* he thought. *Absolutely beautiful.* Suddenly a tinge of insecurity consumed him. He wondered if she was out of his league. He was just a beat cop after all.

Diane glanced at her watch, a petite timepiece with a slender golden band. "Seven p.m. on the nose. I like a man who can come on time," she purred. Or was is a growl? He didn't know or care. All that mattered was that it was working for him.

He picked the nicest place he could afford, a small Italian restaurant with dark mood lighting and a candle on each table. Later, he had no idea what they'd eaten or even much of what they talked about since he could only stare into her eyes.

Diane told him she had dessert waiting back at her house. He quickly flagged down the waiter and paid the check. Even when chasing perps, he didn't drive as fast as he did on the way back to her place.

Before the door was even closed, the two were wrapped in each other's arms, their lips pressed firmly against one another's. Within moments they were in her bedroom. Clothes flew off their bodies onto the floor, and they collapsed on to her bed, intertwined like the threads in a sweater.

Diane's supple, perky breasts heaved against his firm chest as the two of them continued to kiss, more and more wildly. Suddenly, she stopped and sat up. "Did you remember to bring the pepper spray?" she asked.

"In my pants pocket," he joked then wondered if she was serious, if she really had wanted him to bring the spray.

"Oh, that's what that was and I thought my dress wasn't low cut enough," she said with a grin. They shared a laugh as she teased him a bit more, leaning over the side of the bed and grabbing a condom, as Richard studied her glorious ass. "Now we can really get things going," she said as she held up the rubber.

Richard's eyebrow rose a little. She was certainly a woman who knew what she wanted and wasn't afraid to get it. Richard had been with some aggressive women before, but Diane was taking no prisoners. Richard liked a woman who took charge, and Diane certainly did that.

"Maximums, I assumed!" She held up an extra large condom.

"I can try to squeeze myself into one I guess."

They chuckled together, and then Richard showed her he hadn't been kidding about the size.

"Ever been to South America?" She asked. Richard wasn't sure where he was going with this. He clearly looked confused since she followed her statement with, "I hope you enjoy your trip to Brazil."

He stared with delight. *What a woman!*

CHAPTER THIRTEEN

Myles sat in his office, an 80's love song playing on the computer speakers. He hummed along loudly as he worked until the chirp of a text stopped him. It was from Brody. "BUSY LATER?"

Myles typed a reply, "CAN'T. SEEING HUNTER AGAIN."

Diane entered Myles' office and pulled the plug from the speakers. There was blessed silence. She couldn't bear another bad 80's love song pouring through the wall to her office next door. Every time Myles fell in love, he'd blast Phil Collins, Lionel Richie, or Sade. It'd been a week of this crap and Myles humming along. She'd had enough. Besides, it was her turn to talk and she wanted to share some news.

"Why'd you do that?" Myles asked.

"Someone's been getting a lot of WWF smack-down-scream-all night- so-the-neighbors-bang- on-the-wall-style sex."

"It shows?" said he asked coyly. He was slightly embarrassed. The old songs had apparently given him away.

"I'm talking about myself and my spicy Latin lover."

He gave her a big smile. "You and Richard? Last night?"

"It was kind of like a spinning class. Hot and sweaty, but with handcuffs, a nightstick, and pepper spray." She grinned.

"Pepper spray? Okay..." Myles didn't know what to make of her statement, joking or not.

"What about you and Hunter? Judging from your recent playlist of eighties love songs, I'd say it's going pretty well for you too."

Myles noted that she was only too happy to share the news about her and Richard but obviously, craving gossip, as always, she also wanted to hear the details of Myles' love life. The perfect friendship balance.

Myles tapped his computer, and a screensaver of Hunter appeared. "Take a look; tell me what you think." And there was Hunter, dressed in his vest and wife beater, a sexy grin on his face.

Very sexy, Diane thought. Only two weeks and he'd changed his screen-saver to a selfie of himself with his new boy. Myles was again clearly in love. How over-the-top Myles was, she thought. She couldn't help but tease him a little bit about his new crush. "You, my friend, are just an easy-bake oven away from being a twelve-year-old girl, aren't you?"

Myles looked at the shot of him and Hunter and realized, only slightly chagrined, that she was right. But it was fine. He was in love and nothing was going to bother him.

CHAPTER FOURTEEN

It was a tradition in the police station for a more experienced officer to take the new recruits outs for a drink. Part welcoming; part hazing—but all in fun. This time it had been Brody's turn. O'Malley's Pub was their go-to place. Any officer who enjoyed a drink had gotten at least a little tipsy there, if not full-on shit-faced drunk. Brody rolled in like the mayor with the younger officers in tow. One of him and six of them, but he was sure he could out drink all of them.

Brody ordered the first round of beers and shots. The ranking officer paid first. After that the recruits each paid for a round for everyone.

He spent the night regaling them with stories about the force. What to expect. What not to expect. He listed off all the local establishments that offered discounts to cops, as well as where to get the strongest coffee and the best donuts, and how to stay off the Captain's shit list, something he himself was not especially good at.

The next morning, hung over and feeling half sick, Brody entered the gym where Richard was working out on the bench press machine.

"You okay, partner?" he asked Brody.

"I went out with the new recruits last night—to O'Malley's Pub. I'm not sure which are worse to get your drink on at, the gay bars or the Irish ones." He rubbed his eyes with the tips of his fingers. There was a sledgehammer beating inside his head, and he felt completely hung over.

"I guess it depends on what you're looking for at the end of the rainbow," Richard added.

"At this point I'd settle for a well-hung leprechaun," Brody joked as he bent down, adjusted some weights, and began to lift them. His head was splitting and what he needed was a Bloody Mary, but that wasn't going to happen. Couldn't have any suspects smelling his breath.

"That's why I'm glad I'm dating again. I'm in bed by ten p.m."

"If I ever go to sleep at ten, put a bullet in me." Brody was determined to not be one of those guys in their mid thirties who are in bed before midnight no matter how early his morning shift was.

"I'm telling you, this past week has been great, and the sex with Diane is amazing. Which reminds me, I need some more pepper spray."

Brody laughed. "I'm not going to ask. Besides, the visual of Diane having sex is really not something I want in my head for the rest of the day."

"Really? Because I do." Richard winked and flashed his pearly whites at Brody.

"It's been a couple of weeks for Myles too with this new guy he met online. I know because I'm patiently waiting for him to get dumped." Brody grunted as he worked the weights. Actually, he didn't know how he felt about Myles' relationship with this new guy. They'd been together two weeks now, and Myles seemed really happy for the first time in a long time. He was glad for Myles in that the thing with Hunter had lasted at least beyond a first meeting. But could it continue? He hoped it would, he told himself. But if that were true, why was he feeling down? It didn't make sense. He should be happy for his friend.

"Oh, yeah." Richard gave him a strange look. "That's the kind of healthy, positive support a best friend deserves."

The exercise and the booze were making Brody sweat. "Hey. I'm just standing by like I always do…" He lowered the weight to the floor. "…to pick up the pieces when his heart gets broken again."

"Admit it. You miss him."

Brody stood and faced him. "You don't know what you're talking about." He ran an arm across his dripping forehead. He swore he could still smell last night's vodka coming out of his pores. Okay, maybe Richard was right. Maybe he did miss him... a little. Who was he kidding? He missed him a lot. It just wasn't the same when they didn't get together anymore. Brody never thought he'd admit it, but he was lonely. He couldn't remember the last time he'd missed anyone.

"If you say so, but I do know this... if he were my friend and I missed him, I'd pick up a few beers, some Chinese take-out and stop by his house after work to see him."

"Well, you're not me and I don't need your advice." Who did Richard think he was? Brody's mother? He didn't need Richard's advice. It was stupid thing to say, and he was determined to ignore it.

...

Myles was just putting the finishing touches on a perfectly set dinner table. Every dish and every piece of silverware were in place, as were the linen napkins and a silver candelabra. Everything was perfect and soon Hunter would arrive. There was a knock at the door.

"Come in!" The door opened and Brody entered carrying a bag of Chinese food and a six-pack of beer just as Richard had prescribed.

"Brody!" Myles seemed really surprised.

Body wondered why, as he set down the food. "I thought it would be nice if I surprised you with dinner."

"That's so good of you, but I already have plans for tonight."

Brody suddenly noticed the set table for the first time. Beautiful and elegant. Complete with candles and all. It was warming and inviting. Myles' home was the home that he always dreamt that one day he'd have. Oh, man, he'd really screwed up. He was embarrassed that he had assumed Myles would be free. He decided to deflect his disappointment with humor. "I see. Having Liberace over for dinner tonight?" Though he tried to joke about it, he felt dumb, embarrassed. He never should have taken Richard's advice. How was he so out of the loop that he hadn't heard about Myles planning a big evening?

"It's the first time Hunter is coming here. I wanted to do something special." Myles looked a little bummed that Brody wasn't part of the plans for the evening. How awesome of Brody to surprise him with Chinese food. Part of Myles was excited to entertain Hunter this evening, and a quiet part of him would rather it be Brody.

Well, that was that, Brody thought. "Maybe you and I can do something another day then?" In addition to the embarrassment he felt a tinge of regret. What the hell was this? The loner. The guy who didn't need anyone else. Yeah, right. It was a little bit disturbing to find out he had emotions like everyone else. He certainly wasn't going to give in to them. He'd quickly lock them away and ignore them.

"You know you're welcome to stay and join us." It sounded awkward but it was a sincere invitation from Myles.

"Don't be ridiculous. I don't do threesomes," Brody fired back.

"Since when?"

They both laughed as Myles glanced at the table. "Too much isn't it?"

"No." Brody looked into Myles' eyes. "It's excessive and over-the-top, but it's you. That's what I think is so nice about it. Other guys may find it terrifying, but I think it's wonderful." And he did because Myles tried so hard to please. And that was a good thing. Except Brody wished he didn't try so hard that he set himself up for a fall.

"You like that about me?"

"That you're psycho? Of course. It makes me look normal." Brody paused for a moment. "Look, finish getting ready. We'll get together tomorrow, okay?"

"Happy hour?"

Brody smiled. "Sure." He looked across the table at Myles in his apron and with an oven mitt in hand. The perfect husband to someone who was smart enough to realize what a great guy he really was.

. . .

Well that was a dumb waste of time and effort, Brody thought as he exited Myles' apartment and sat in his car with his Chinese food in hand.

What the hell, Brody thought. He might as well make use of some of the food he'd bought. He had nowhere to go and the food was fresh and hot now. Might as well eat it here, he told himself. He opened a container of Kung Pao chicken, pulled a plastic fork from the bag it came in and began to eat. He really shouldn't have shown up at Myles' place unannounced. He should have known Myles and the new guy –... what was his name? Hunter. Yeah sure, it was—would be getting together for one of Myles' fabulous dinners sooner or later.

He glanced up at Myles' apartment, pulled out his cell and launched the Grindr app. The image of a man who said his name was Stone appeared on the screen. Yeah, about as likely a name as Hunter. What did he care? He'd probably never see the guy again anyhow. Brody was lonely and wanted someone to be with. This guy fit the bill and lived close by.

He didn't care who it really was, just another nameless guy. It was just a quick "blow and go" for Brody. He quickly took a few more bites of his food and washed it down with a beer. *Let's do this,* he thought to himself as he started the car and headed into the night.

Shortly afterward, Brody pulled up outside Stone's apartment. The door opened to reveal a slender, attractive man dressed in a vintage CBGB tee shirt and black skinny jeans. "Hey, I'm Stone."

"Brody. Nice to meet you."

"Come in. Can I get you a beer?"

"Sure. Looks like you've done this before."

"Maybe once or twice." He smirked, indicating that they both knew that they had done this many times before. He closed the door as Brody stepped inside.

. . .

Myles finished setting up the liquor bottles as he put the finishing touches on everything. He looked at the clock on the wall. It was seven on the dot. He took off his apron, hung it on a hook in the kitchen, and walked to the bathroom where he turned on the shower. He hoped things turned out okay. As usual, he'd done his best. But there was always that nagging little doubt. Had he forgotten anything?

"Shit!" he said aloud. "I forgot the ice." He'd draw a quick bath and then call Hunter and ask him to bring some with him.

. . .

Brody appraised the other man and liked what he saw. "So how do you want to do this?"

"Quickly. I've got dinner in an hour."

"I'm okay with being an appetizer."

The man smiled and pulled off his shirt revealing a lean sculpted body with just the right amount of chest hair .

"Just so you know," Brody told him, "you may be late for dessert."

"Fine by me."

Brody shed his own shirt, and the two of them kissed and headed quickly to the bedroom where they fell into bed ready for a quick hot fuck. Then the man's phone rang.

"Ignore it," he said. "It's probably just my date tonight. He's obsessive compulsive."

"How annoying."

"Right!" he agreed, as they reached for each other and the phone continued to ring.

"I can't," Brody said not wanting to be annoyed by an overbearing date determined to talk to the guy he's about to have sex with. "Just get it."

"I'll send it to voice-mail." He pulled the phone from his pocked and pressed a button, but not before Brody thought he saw Myles' picture on the phone's caller ID. *Oh, shit,* he thought. This *was not* possible. "Please tell me your name's not Hunter."

"Of course, it isn't."

"Good. Whew." He lay back.

"Hunter's a hook-up name… like Stone."

Brody quickly sat up. *Damn it,* he thought. Out of all the guys on Grindr! What the hell were the odds of this? "Oh, fuck me." This couldn't be happening. Of all the men in L.A. Shit!

"Sure," Hunter answered, "If you want me to top."

"No. I mean as in: 'God damn it'." Brody felt a tightness in his throat. How could this happen?

"What's the problem?"

"That's my best friend! Damn! I really wanted you to turn out to be a good guy."

"I am a good guy." He paused, considering. "Well, maybe not marriage material."

"I gotta go." Frantic, he jumped from the bed and strode to the living room, followed by Hunter. Quickly, he pulled on his clothes trying to process what had just happened and how he'd explain it to Myles.

At the front door Hunter grabbed his arm. Brody was hot and Hunter was horny. Why was he freaking out? Hunter wanted to play around a bit and they still had plenty of time.

"Chill out. This is no big deal."

Now Brody was really pissed. This guy was leading Myles on and didn't even care about him. Damn it. "Actually it is. Myles is going to freak out when he hears that I almost slept with his boyfriend."

"Boyfriend? We're not boyfriends. Myles is a nice guy and a decent lay, but that's about where it ends."

"Don't make me knock you out." It had been a long time since Brody had been this angry. Brody's fears had just been actualized. Myles had fallen for a guy who didn't give a shit about him and was about to break his heart again.

"Hey. You're in my house, remember?" he warned, starting to get angry.

"Listen! This is the way it's going to happen. You go have dinner tonight with Myles and don't say a word about this. It never happened." Brody was in damage control mode. If nothing else, he'd try to contain the damage that this would cause.

"You know what? Why don't you get out? I'm serious. Now."

"I'm not done here." Broody seethed.

"Actually, yes you are. And if you don't go, I'll call the cops."

Body laughed in his face while taking an aggressive stance. "I *am* a cop."

"Well if that's the case, then I'll call Myles and tell him that I just hooked up with his best friend... the cop."

Brody let out a long breath he didn't know he'd been holding. He could clearly see that this was escalating into a no-win situation for him. If it was going to get settled, it would have to be through diplomacy. This guy was unfortunately holding all the cards and Brody knew that he could be the big loser in this situation.

"Okay. Relax. I'll go, but you have to agree not to be an asshole to Myles. Be cool, have dinner with him tonight and don't say a word about this, okay? I'm asking nicely." He figured Hunter's listening to him was about as certain as a foot of snow in L.A. but he had to try to settle this amicably.

Damn it; he still couldn't believe this was the same man Myles had been raving about. The perfect one. The one he was sure he'd spend the rest of his life with. He was a creep and Brody was holding back from just punching his lights out.

"See? Now you're being a good boy." He looked directly into Brody's eyes mocking him. "But just so you know... I'll do what I want. I'm going to start with throwing you out of my apartment. You got it?"

"I got it," he murmured as he bit down on his tongue and tried to contain his rage.

"Good. I'm glad we're on the same page again. Now leave!" Hunter held the door open as Brody walked outside. He gave Brody a shove and then slammed the door behind him. "Asshole," Brody heard Hunter say just as he was saying the very same thing.

. . .

Myles, wrapped in a towel as he exited the shower, was just going to get dressed when the text arrived. It was from Hunter. "I'm not coming tonight. I'm not into it." Not again! He felt himself deflate like a helium balloon losing air.

Damn it, he couldn't believe it, not after all the trouble he'd gone to, after the dinner he'd prepared. Everything perfect, plus all the time it took. All the special little touches. What did he do wrong? He couldn't comprehend where he screwed up this time. He had been extra careful not to smother him. He attempted to avoid all the mistakes in the past that scared off all the other guys. It was different with Hunter.

Myles heart sank in his chest. He'd screwed it up again. There was no denying it. He was broken. Something was wrong with him and for the life of him, he couldn't figure out what it was. Feeling totally defeated, he picked up the phone and dialed Brody's number. He needed someone to make him feel okay about himself. He was feeling lower than he had felt in a very long time. This was it, he thought. This was his last chance at finding love. Brody was the only person who could put a smile on his face at a time like this.

CHAPTER FIFTEEN

Brody entered his apartment and flopped on the couch. This was a disaster. What had he done? What if Myles found out? He couldn't imagine what kind of overreaction he'd get about this. Myles didn't understand things like casual sex and just hooking up. He knew he'd read into it and accuse him of the hookup being something more than a simple misunderstanding. Brody also knew that if he found out that Hunter wasn't interested in him the way Myles thought he was, it would break his heart. Either way it was a no-win situation for Brody and he didn't know what to do.

He sat on the couch contemplating how to handle the situation should it come up. As these thoughts raced through Brody's head, the phone rang. He dreaded finding out who was on the line. Yet he knew instinctively who it was. He pulled the phone out of his pocket and looked at it. Of course, it was Myles. Brody braced himself for the worst as he picked up the phone. *Time to pay the piper,* he thought. Brody picked up.

"Hunter broke up with me," Myles blurted out in the saddest voice Brody had ever heard him use.

"Aw, shit. I'm so sorry. Myles." Did Myles not know what happened? Did Hunter just break it off and not say anything? Brody could tell by Myles' voice that that he had dodged a bullet, and maybe he was off the hook with having to tell Myles what happened.

"Could you come over?" He couldn't stand being alone. He'd really thought this was the one.

"Death by chocolate?"

"Death by homemade tiramisu." He tried his best to keep the mood light so as to not scare Brody off. He knew if he sounded too morose that Brody wouldn't want to come and listen to his complaining. But he knew that even at the worst of melodramatic moments, Brody was always there for him. Tonight Myles really wanted to see him and was determined not to fuck things up.

"Be right there," Brody answered. What to do? Should he tell Myles what happened? Own up to it so there were no secrets between them? Or should he just let it go and hope Myles never found out? Okay, he thought, he'd play it by ear. Either way, dessert was on the table. More important, he had his best friend back, and that made him happy.

On the ride over to Myles' apartment, Brody's anger broiled. What a dick this Hunter guy was. How could he do that to a nice guy like Myles? If only there was a law against lying on Grindr, he would have hauled the asshole into the station.

But he had to put that out of his mind now. He still needed to decide if he was going to tell Myles what had happened. Brody had never lied to Myles about anything and had promised himself that he never would. How could he break this to his friend? Brody had never cheated on anyone.

Cheating was the one thing that crossed all boundaries and violated all the rules. He had known the pain of being lied to and cheated on and swore he would never do that to another person. Never allow someone to feel that pain because of him. Thus, he had one-night stands with strangers so he never had to worry about it. Myles, on the other hand, was loving, caring, honest, and true, the patron saint of gay dating. Any guy would be lucky to be with him, and that ass Hunter didn't know what he had.

. . .

Myles and Brody sat at the impeccably set dining room table. French press coffee, homemade tiramisu, flowers, the whole bit. Myles melancholy. He was being so sweet that Brody couldn't help but try to make him feel better.

"One day you're going to find a guy who is smart enough to realize what an amazing catch you are," Brody said as he sat at a table dressed so perfectly that Martha Stewart herself would be envious of. "You're going to make someone the best husband."

"What about you?" Myles asked, subtly inferring that the invitation was there should Brody be interested.

"Me?" Myles had to be kidding, Brody thought, a hint of regret in his voice. "I'm no catch." Lost in his own guilt, he'd totally missed the inflection in Myles' voice indicating that the question he posed was an invitation and not an inquiry as to his own virtues as a partner.

"That's not true," Myles answered. Did Brody really feel that way? How could he? He was always so confidant, so self-assured. He had to know deep down in his heart that any guy would be lucky to have his love.

He took a bite of the dessert. "Yes, it is. I'm not like you. Any guy who would pass up a night like this with you is a fool."

"Well... I'm obviously doing something wrong." It was sweet of Brody to think that someone would be fortunate to have a man like Myles as a husband, but even Brody didn't want him in that way. Myles was determined not to make this a pity party. He just wanted to enjoy what was left of the evening with his friend, resolved that it was not going to take a downward turn.

"It's the guys. You just have lousy taste in men. Like Hunter for example..." Brody thought he'd approach the subject carefully. He wanted to tell Myles what happened. It was the right thing to do.

"Let's not talk about him, okay? I'm depressed enough without talking about him. He was nothing but a jerk, an asshole, if the truth be told. Besides, I don't want to ruin the rest of the night talking about him."

"I think we should..." Brody insisted, once again attempting to come clean with what had happened.

"I really don't want to." Myles firmly snapped back. "Hunter is over and done with. It's time to forget him."

"Let me finish. He doesn't deserve you. Any guy who would break up with you by text is a creep and isn't worth your time." This was Brody's last attempt to share with Myles what happened earlier in the evening.

"You don't think I know that? I didn't even call him back. I'm tired of being mistreated by guys who don't appreciate me." It's said that depression comes from anger. If so, the depression was turning back to the original. He was damned angry now. He was tired of trying so hard and having it end by being ditched.

"Good for you Myles." Could it be that his friend was finally learning to love himself? Myles needed to stand-up for who he was and accept all the gifts he had to offer. Brody was pleased that Myles was taking charge of his life and demanding that men respect him.

"Now, can we please just move on? Let's just enjoy the fact that we're hanging out together," Myles asserted in a strong confident tone that Brody barely recognized.

"Sure. Let's make tonight about your amazing dessert."

"And us!"

CHAPTER SIXTEEN

Brody and Richard sat on the hood of their squad car eating lunch from a taco truck.

"So run this by me one more time," Richard said. "Why didn't you tell him what happened the other night with this Hunter guy?"

Brody shrugged, feeling miserable. "I couldn't. If you knew how upset he'd be, you wouldn't have told him either."

"Actually, yes, I would have." Richard's tone was stern.

"Myles can't handle these things."

"He's a grown man."

"On the outside maybe, but on the inside he's all Hello Kitty. Plus, he'll never find out." Or at least Brody hoped he wouldn't. Anyway, how could he? Brody wasn't going to tell him, and Hunter or Stone—whoever the hell he said he was—wouldn't either, now that he was out of the picture.

"That's not how it works. They always find out. Trust me. And if they don't, you'll always think in the back of your head that they know and just aren't saying anything."

"Does someone have some baggage from a past relationship they want to talk about?"

Richard chuckled humorously. "Let's just say I learned the hard way." Brody knew him all too well.

"Fine. I'll talk to him." Brody knew Richard was right. He hated to admit it–and wouldn't. He and Myles had a relationship based on trust and honesty, and he wasn't going to let that change. No matter how hard it would be.

As soon as they finished eating, Brody called and asked Myles to meet him at the go-go bar. For a night of drinking.

...

It was happy hour. Heavy house music thumped as Myles sat with his Manhattan. Brody was late. Strange, Myles thought. Brody, much like Myles, was always on time. It was one of the few things that they shared in common. It was one of those little idiosyncrasies he loved about Brody, laid back but always punctual. They both felt that it was passive aggressive to make someone wait for you, a trait they hated in people. Something must have come up, Myles surmised, and he was happy to wait.

Finally Brody arrived and took a seat beside him.

"Hey, Myles. How you doing?" Without a doubt Brody was not looking forward to telling Myles what had happened. In fact, he'd delayed showing up for that very reason. Now, he just had to hope it would be okay.

"It's my second Manhattan, so pretty good." He joked. It was his way of letting Brody know that he wasn't upset that he was twenty minutes late.

"Are you still upset about Hunter?"

"I liked him. He was a really nice guy." His voice sounded sad but not angry or depressed like it had before.

Brody gave him an earnest look. "He wasn't that nice." Brody thought he'd broach the subject slowly. Warm Myles up to what he had to tell him.

The bartender approached them. He was clearly familiar with Brody and his choice of drink "Hi, Brody. Martini?"

"No. Thanks. I'll just get it thrown in my face."

The bartender frowned in puzzlement. After a moment he shrugged and left.

"What did you do?" Myles asked, his tone full of apprehension. He knew Brody all too well and this was clearly going to be something big that Brody had to get off his chest.

"Can we just start off by me saying it wasn't my fault?" He felt a knot in his stomach. This was harder than he thought it would be.

Myles couldn't imagine Brody doing anything so wrong that he'd actually be that upset with him. He figured that he'd just make light of the news Brody was about to deliver. He teased. "That's the worst way to start a conversation! That's like telling someone, 'Oh. I know it looks bad,' or, 'This is just going to hurt a little bit.'"

Brody took a deep breath. He knew he had to get this over with and just hope for the best. "I can already tell this is not going to end well."

"I've known you for over ten years. Nothing you can say is going to bother or surprise me anymore. So just tell me." Myles hated games. He was a lawyer, so he just wanted facts. He knew Brody fucked up and had something to confess. He just wanted to know what happened and move on. No need to dance around it. Myles knew all of Brody's tricks by now.

If that would only be true, Brody thought. But he had his doubts. "I ran Hunter's ID down at the station. His real name is Steven Adams. He's from Nebraska."

"I know where he's from. But I didn't know his name wasn't Hunter." Brody watched Myles process that and brace for whatever he had to say. Myles tone was shifted from amusement to genuine annoyance.

Okay, Brody thought. This was going to be the hard part. Yes, he'd known Myles for years, but he didn't know how he'd react. "Yeah and it's not Stone either. That's the point."

"What's the point? And who is Stone?"

"Exactly! Neither of us knew his real name." Damn it, this was hard, Brody thought.

Myles frowned. "Just tell me what happened."

It was now or never, but he really had no choice. "The other night after I left your place I went on Grindr to meet someone."

"You hooked up with Hunter!" Brody dropped the bomb and Myles was ground zero. Did he just hear correctly?!

"I didn't know it was Hunter! He called himself Stone. Who calls himself that anyways? He texted me on Grindr, and I went to his house. I didn't know I was doing anything wrong. I would never do that to you!"

"You suck." Myles dismissed him. It was like a switch had been turned off within him.

Oh, crap, Brody thought. He was afraid of this. Now Myles was both hurt and angry. Again, Brody should not have taken Richard's advice. Would he never learn? "How was I supposed to know? You've never introduced me to the guy."

"So you were the one who ruined this for me? I met a great guy and you just couldn't stand it, could you?"

This was even worse than he'd thought it might be. Damn it, why did he have to hook up with the same man as Myles? Karma? Fate? Whatever? Shit! Well, maybe Myles had a right to be upset. But my God, Brody hadn't known it was Hunter.

"He's not a great guy. Certainly not the Prince Charming you think he is. Trust me, Hunter's a creep."

"Trust you?" Myles was furious. He suspected that Brody was jealous that he wasn't spending time with him. Myles knew that Brody missed him and needed his attention, but this? Total betrayal! Myles felt like he was just sucker punched in the gut. His best friend stabbed him in the back. Brody clearly wanted out of their "Ten Year Plan" and went to great extents to weasel out of the arrangement. That had hurt Myles' feelings, but he was willing to let that go because he knew Brody wasn't capable of having an adult relationship, but to sabotage Myles' chances of happiness, just so that he always had a buddy to hang out with, crossed the line.

Brody had just hurt Myles like no one had ever hurt him before. He trusted that they had each other's best interest in mind, but clearly Brody was too selfish to give a fuck about Myles' happiness. Myles snapped right then and there. The rest of the conversation was a large buzz in his ears. Myles contained his rage and looked for the cleanest exit.

Brody was becoming angry too. Why was Myles overreacting? It was a simple mistake. Why did Brody have to be the one to pay for all the guys who had hurt him in the past? Myles was the one who set himself up by overdoing it on every date he went on. Myles needed to accept his responsibility in all of it. "Think about it Myles. It's always the same thing. You bring this on yourself. Stop hoping that one man is going to be what you need to make you happy. That's not the case. It never will be. Face it Myles, there is no knight in shining armor who'll come for you. There never will be." Brody couldn't believe he'd said that but there was no taking the words back.

"Sadly that's true, isn't it?" Abruptly, Myles stood up. "Things can't stay the same. I've got to go. Sorry, Brody, but I can't do this anymore." Myles wasn't going to engage with this anymore.

He agreed with Brody. He was partially responsible. He had indeed blindly trusted every guy he went out with and wore his heart on his sleeve. This was the very last straw. It ended now. No one was going to hurt him anymore. Especially Brody. After ten years of hoping something special existed between them, Myles need to accept the simple truth. It didn't. Not in that way. Brody was incapable of giving Myles the love and relationship he wanted. It needed to end now.

Brody had badly wounded him. He didn't want to even look at him. Myles hurt so deeply that it took all of his strength and self-control to manage to be civil when leaving the bar.

"Wait. What?" Brody was shocked. God, what had he done!

Myles looked at Brody with sadness. He called to the bartender and threw down a couple of bills. He wanted to make a statement. A farewell gesture. This would be the last time he saw Brody. He would buy him a drink and exit his life forever. He turned to the bartender who could see that things had gone very wrong between these two men.

Myles calmly ordered. "A martini... DIRTY!" he said, indicating that what Brody had done was reprehensible, then he stood and strode toward the door, and never looked back.

"Myles, please—" Brody called after him, but before he could finish, Myles was gone.

And Brody knew that things would never be the same.

CHAPTER SEVENTEEN

Parked at the side of the road in their squad car, Brody, with a dark cloud over his head, and Richard were looking for speeders. Sure enough, a car soon came by that set off the radar.

"Look at this guy," Richard said. "He didn't even attempt to slow down when he saw us."

"Light 'em up." Brody was really pissed—not at the driver but at the situation with Myles. He couldn't do anything about that. But he could about this.

"He was just going forty."

"He's speeding. Right in front of us! People need to learn respect for authority. *Light 'em up*. Let's get him!" Brody knew he was overreacting but couldn't control how he felt.

"It's not a big deal." Richard tried to dismiss the situation. Brody had been a nightmare to deal with all week. He'd been edgy and irritated. Not the lovable, fun partner Richard enjoyed, but a sullen, depressed mess of a man who was riding Richard's last nerve.

Brody gave Richard an icy look. "I said *let's get him*."

"Are you now the asshole cop who chases down an '87 Corolla for going fifteen miles over the speed limit?"

"Yes," he snapped back, quickly adjusting his tone with Richard, knowing he'd totally overreacted and a bit embarrassed at his behavior.

"You really need to straighten this thing out with Myles."

"I've tried calling, texting, and e-mailing. He's not talking to me. I may not be the smartest guy around, but I can take a hint when someone doesn't want to see me." Richard could hear the desperation in his voice.

"You need to go over there and work this out. Knock his door down if you have to."

Brody ignored him. Richard didn't know Myles like he did. Once Myles made his mind up about something, there was no changing it. Myles was hurt and done with Brody, and he knew that. No amount of apologizing could fix what had happened between them.

"You're a cop for Christ's sake. Man up! You miss him. Make it right."

"He's not going to forgive me," Brody attempted to explain to Richard, despite knowing that it was pointless.

"You owe it to yourself and even more so, you owe it to Myles to clear this up. It was an innocent mistake; you can't let him go on hurting like this. If not for your sake, for Myles' sake. He doesn't deserve the heartache this is bringing him."

Richard was right. Just like he was during lunch when he told Brody to make sure he confessed everything right away. Brody couldn't let Myles go through the rest of his life thinking that his best friend betrayed him. He knew he had to talk to Myles whether he wanted to or not.

. . .

That night after work Brody pulled up in front of Myles' apartment. He wasn't sure about how this would go. *Come on, man,* he told himself. *Myles is your friend. Your best friend and has been for years.* He sighed deeply, *you have to do this. He deserves to know the truth.* Brody paused for a moment, and then climbed out of the car.

Inside the apartment building Brody banged at the door. No answer. He tried again. "Myles? I know you're in there. Please answer. Please talk to me. I need you to open up now."

Across the hall, Mr. Harrington opened his door. "Knock one more time and I'm calling the cops."

Brody turned and flashed his badge. He was in no mood for this guy and just wanted to shut him up.

"Sorry, officer. Undercover, huh? A sting operation? I get it! Is everything okay? Are you still after Myles?"

Not this guy again, Brody thought. "Have you seen him?"

The man shook his head. "What did he do this time?"

"He didn't do anything." The guy was a jerk! No, he was just the typical nosey neighbor. He had to stop blaming everyone else for his own problems.

"It's always the quiet ones. I knew he was a bad seed!" Mr. Harrington said.

"That isn't the case," Brody said, his tone dismissive.

"Of course you can't say anything. I know what's going on. I just hope you get that son-of-a bitch!" Mr. Harrington expounded as he gave a nervous look around the courtyard, obviously wanting to see if any additional mischief was afoot. With a look of satisfaction that all was fine, he retreated into his apartment.

Brody shook his head at the obviously off fellow and realized Myles wasn't home. He'd have to try another day. Defeated, but slightly relieved, he left the complex.

. . .

Myles sat on the couch in Diane's house with a full spread of food in front of him—not the sort he would generally eat, but the situation had changed. Diane was his only friend now and the only person who he could talk to and share his news with. He was thankful to have her in his life. If it weren't for her, he'd have nobody. Diane's house was a homey place with comfortable chairs and couch, in a warm brown. Splotches of color—abstract art—decorated three walls. The fourth wall was a large picture window looking out on a wide expanse of green lawn.

Diane entered the living room carrying two beers proclaiming, "Pizza, wings, and beer. Who needs men?" She set the drinks on the coffee table in front of the couch. "We'll have more fun without them."

Myles rolled his eyes. "No, we won't."

She half-shrugged and admitted, "You're right."

Myles took a swig of beer. "I'll try not to bitch about how much men suck." It was meant to be funny, but behind the humor was a bit of truth.

There was all the bad luck he'd had in dating, and now this thing with Brody. Of course, he had to admit it really wasn't all Brody's fault, Hunter hooked up with him too. They were both to blame, he thought. But no, that wasn't fair either. Brody had no idea that Hunter and Stone were the same person.

If he was being honest with himself, the truth was that Myles didn't care enough about Hunter for it to really hurt. It was Brody who had broken his heart this time. If Brody had cared, he wouldn't have hooked up with anyone that night. No, that wasn't true either. But Myles couldn't stop blaming Brody and himself for being so gullible, and for believing that something existed between them for all those years. He sighed and shook his head.

"Lucky for you, I have the perfect evening planned. Comfort food, ice cream, and a romantic movie!" She pulled out a copy of her favorite romantic comedy, *eCupid.*

"I love that we're doing this," Myles said. And he did very much appreciate that Diane was there when he needed her.

"I do it every day."

"What about Richard?"

"Are you kidding me? He's more into it than I am. Two bowls of pistachio ice cream, twin snuggies, and a romantic movie. We cry all night long!" She laughed at Myles' expression.

"Lucky bitch."

"I know."

"Diane, I need to tell you something. Please don't be upset." Despite what he asked, Myles knew she would be. But after a great deal of thought he'd come to a decision, the only logical one there was. Now was the time to spring it on her.

"Any conversation that starts with 'don't be upset' upsets me." Diane knew Myles was going to spring something big on her. He was acting unusually pensive.

"I need to start fresh. Go somewhere far away from here." There, it was out. It felt good to finally tell her. He'd been struggling with this decision and how to let her know about it for days.

"You're moving to the Valley?"

"I'm thinking of transferring to the New York office. There's a job opening for a senior litigator that starts next week. I know you're not going to agree with this, but I really need to be anywhere but here."

He thought a fresh start was sure to help. He could shed his old personality and become someone different. Not a victim of romance anymore, or so he told himself. He hoped Diane would understand and support him in this decision. It was the right thing to do. Myles was convinced of it. He had struggled with this decision all week and had finally reached the most practical of solutions.

"You want to leave and move to New York?" And there was staid and fierce Diana, with tears about to spill from her eyes. Was she hearing correctly? Was Myles really going to bail on everything he had because of this?

"We both know I should go."

"Actually, *we* don't. I think you're running away from your problems." She attempted to be understanding but was failing miserably at it.

"Please don't make this harder for me than it already is. I need to do this." He'd made up his mind and was determined to follow through. Of course, he had regrets, but what he planned to do was for the best.

"No you don't. It's an irrational, impetuous... and a totally emotionally-clouded decision."

"I have to break this cycle, and I can't do it in Los Angeles." He'd miss Diane and his life in Los Angeles. And then there was Brody—his very best friend for all those years. But he had to do it. It was the best decision for both of them. Brody wouldn't be able to find someone either. They had to stop being each other's crutch. Both of them deserved to find the right person and neither of them could do that with the other interfering in that. His leaving was not only for himself, but for Brody as well. The problem was how to tell Brody that.

He knew that telling Brody would be the worst part. How he was going to do it, he didn't know. But he couldn't just leave without telling him. Or could he? Myles struggled with that decision, as well. Brody deserved to know that Myles was leaving, but Myles wasn't ready to talk to him. Not by a long shot.

"Fine, I'll concede. But only under one condition." Diane wanted to cry but didn't. She'd put on a good game face and make light of the situation. She loved Myles. He was one of her most cherished friends and colleagues. Losing him would hurt, but she understood his need to leave this town and start anew.

Hollywood was a tough place to find love. Myles certainly had tried for the last fifteen years without any success. Maybe New York was the place for him. There they were straightforward, honest, and nonsense wasn't tolerated. All of these were things that could serve Myles well in his quest for happiness.

He tried to lighten the mood. "Let the negotiations begin."

"You have to let me have a going away party for you this weekend," she insisted. This was something that she needed to do, more for her than for Myles.

"Absolutely not. No party. I want a clean break," he told her, "not a maudlin dragging out of things."

"Just a few friends at my place for drinks?"

Okay, maybe he owed it to her, he thought. "No more than six," he insisted.

"Deal." She attempted a smile to let him know things were okay between them but couldn't help but think about what he was going to do about Brody. She carefully broached the subject, curious as to what Myles' plan was to share this news with his best friend for over ten years. "So when are you going to tell Brody that you're heading to the other side of the country?"

Myles paused, obviously considering the question. "I don't know yet."

Since that night at the go-go bar, he'd avoided Brody. Surprisingly, he wasn't mad at him anymore. He couldn't be. Brody was just being Brody, the scared little boy in a man's body, playing "cops and robbers". Like the rest of us, Brody was damaged. Myles knew that all too well. Brody's way of dealing was jumping from bed to bed to avoid his feelings. Myles way of dealing with it was to smother someone with love in hopes they'd be capable of returning a small portion of it.

Myles wasn't angry; he just was disappointed, mostly with himself. He had been lying to both of them for ten years thinking that he and Brody had something special. Secretly, had always wished that Brody would love him like he loved Brody, and that they would eventually be a couple. Myles now knew that day would never come and that he'd been lying, not only to himself but also to Brody about their relationship. The only fair thing to do was to move away, far away for both their sakes.

Diane took a long sip of beer and looked at Myles as if she had a solution to the dilemma of how to break the news to Brody. She gave Myles an impish grin and half jokingly suggested, "I could have Richard tell Brody."

Myles took a drink himself and wondered if that wasn't a half-bad idea.

CHAPTER EIGHTEEN

Brody didn't show up at the station at the start his shift. This was not a rarity anymore. In the past few weeks it had happened again and again. Richard usually solved the problem by calling Brody and waking him up after a late night of drinking or playing video games. But today was worse. Brody didn't answer his phone, so Richard thought best to check on him and see if he was really okay.

Richard banged on the door of Brody's apartment to no avail. He paused and banged again. With his foot he lifted up the doormat to reveal a key underneath. Richard raised his eyes toward heaven.

"And to think he's a cop."

He opened the door and went inside. Brody, half-naked, lay on the couch unconscious. Richard laughed to himself at how ridiculous his partner looked. He was tempted to take a photo on his phone and show it to the guys at the station, but why kick a man when he's down? Richard glanced around, and spotted a ski pole. He picked it up and punched the smoke detector button on the ceiling. The alarm sounded loud and shrill.

Brody opened his eyes, which weren't focused yet on Richard or anything else and instantly panicked. He sprang up only to find Richard in uniform, laughing at his absurdity.

Richard shook his head. "If you were a horse, I'd be obliged to put you down."

Brody looked at him and whinnied like a stallion, indicating an invitation to do so.

He looked like he had a terrible hangover and would welcome being put out of his misery. "What time is it? Am I late?"

"Let's just say you're early for lunch. Why don't you get in the shower?"

Brody stood, yawned, and rubbed his eyes. He was indeed exceedingly late, but he didn't care. In fact, within the past couple of weeks, he didn't care about anything. It was like he'd lost his will to go on. He didn't understand it, all he knew was that he was miserable.

"So, how long is this going to go on?" Richard asked, obviously weary of his partner's shenanigans.

"Five minutes. Let me just rinse off."

"Not the shower, for heaven's sake. The self-pity, the depression. It's been every night this week."

"I've finally found something I'm good at, and I've almost mastered it." His tone was self-mocking. "Why stop short of the finish line?"

"Well, since you're already down, I've got something else for you. It's an invitation." Why not just get this over with? Diane had blackmailed him into telling Brody that Myles was leaving by inviting him to the going away party. Richard fought tooth and nail to get out of having to do this to his partner, but Diane was a relentless litigator, and he knew that he was no match for the leverage she had over him sexually.

"Who from?"

Richard knew Brody had few friends—Diane, himself, and Myles. So no wonder he looked puzzled.

"Diane. She's having people over."

Suddenly Brody was paying strict attention. "Will Myles be there?" Brody smiled for the first time in a week.

Richard was glad to see his partner happy. "Yup."

Wow, Brody thought. This was his chance to reason with Myles, to try to work things out. "This will be the perfect opportunity for me to talk to Myles and set things straight."

"In theory," Richard replied, as vaguely as he could.

Maybe he could invite Brody to the party without letting him know what it was for? Richard certainly didn't want to work the day today with Brody reacting to the news that Myles was moving to New York. Richard knew if he played his cards right and worded this conversation carefully, he'd not only get out of having to be the one to break the bad news to Richard, but he'd finally be able to get Brody and Myles in a room together where he hoped they would work things out. Richard proceeded carefully with his choice of words.

"Was this Diane's idea?" Brody asked. Maybe she'd set this up just to bring the two of them together. If so, that was great.

"Absolutely! So you'll come?"

"Of course! Now I've got something to look forward to." Brody now had a renewed sense of purpose.

"Me too," Richard answered sardonically.

. . .

A small group of friends and co-workers stood around a table in the dining room in Diane's house. On the table sat a round cake that read "Bon Voyage." In the corner Richard was making a miserable attempt at tending bar, something he'd obviously never done before. Myles and Diane stood near the others from the office.

"I kept it small like you wanted," Diane told him.

Myles knew she was proud of the affair she was throwing on his behalf. It wasn't the small gathering they agreed to, but Myles knew the moment that they made their agreement that Diane had no intention with following through with her promise of a small intimate gathering.

Suddenly, it felt like his heart was melting. "I'll miss you."

"I'm well aware," she answered, playfully trying to mask the sadness she was feeling at the loss of her best friend. Then more seriously: "I still can't believe you're doing this, and driving no less."

"I need to. Plus, five days on the open road will do me well." He tried to convince himself.

"Wait till you hit Nevada. You'll regret that decision all the way to the Statue of Liberty," she joked.

Myles felt sadness too, but he was determined to search his soul on this trip and hopefully find what he needed.

Richard walked toward them with two drinks and a panicked expression. He'd failed to tell Diane and Myles that he hadn't fully delivered the message that Myles was leaving. He merely invited Brody to the party. He knew there would be fallout and didn't want to be anywhere close by when the explosion occurred. "Brody's here. I'll be in the bomb shelter if anyone's looking for me," he said, as he attempted to retreat to the furthest corners of the house.

"Oh, no," said Diane, clasping his arm and he could tell she wasn't going to let him slip away. He felt, in fact, like a puppy that had just piddled on the carpet. He realized she was going to keep him close by to make sure he didn't get away with anything. "You're not leaving us alone. We need someone here who can handle a firearm."

Brody entered the room. "Hey! Hi." He cheerfully greeted everyone, happy to be invited and excited to resolve the conflict between him and Myles.

"Hey," Myles answered, his voice less than enthusiastic. He wondered why Brody was as happy as he was. Could it be that he agreed with Myles' decision that leaving was the best thing for both of them?

Brody gave Diane a smile. "Thanks for inviting me. It's so good to see you." He paused as he looked from Diane to Myles. "So, what's the occasion? Myles? Did you get a promotion?"

Myles was in shock. After a moment he glanced at Richard, who stood by the bar with a guilty look on his face.

Diane stared at him too. "Richard," she demanded, "will you help me, dear? Oh and bring a shovel." She turned to Myles and Brody.

"Would you excuse us? He's going be busy for a while digging a six by three foot, very deep hole out back." She grabbed Richard's arm and pulled him away like a child caught red-handed toward the kitchen.

Brody looked puzzled. "What was that about?" With Richard's attempted escape and Brody's good cheer, Myles knew that Brody had no idea why he was there. Richard had invited him to a party, and that was all. It was Myles' job now to break the news to him in a roomful of people. Myles was annoyed at Richard, but he knew he had no cause to be. It was his job to do this and no one else's. It had been wrong of him to ask Diane to leverage Richard into doing the dirty deed for him. Myles swallowed hard and tried to deliver the news as best he could to Brody.

"It's just that this isn't exactly a party for my promotion."

"You didn't get promoted?" Brody was confused.

"Technically I did... I guess you could say that."

"That's great. Congrats."

"It's also a going away party."

"Who for?" Brody looked around the room, and it suddenly dawned on him. "You're the one who's leaving." He sounded incredulous. "Where are you going? When are you leaving?" Brody tried to wrap his head around what he was hearing. Was this some kind of prank or bad joke? He looked around to see if anyone else was in on the gag, but no one seemed to be. Just Myles standing inches away from him with eyes swelling up, obviously upset at delivering the soul-crushing news to his friend.

Brody had no idea what to make of this. He knew Myles was mad at him, but leaving him for good? Moving away so he'd never have to see him again? It all felt so surreal. Could this really be happening? He felt as if he was still in a drunken haze.

"I'm heading out Saturday morning. Driving cross country to New York." Myles said with puppy dog eyes.

Brody suddenly looked weak, as if maybe he should sit down. "Saturday? New York?"

Myles nodded sheepishly.

"And this is how you tell me?" Brody suddenly became angry. How dare he break the news to him like this in front of all these people at a party!

"Richard was going to tell you."

"You asked Richard to tell me?" He couldn't believe this.

"Diane did." Myles was suddenly very angry with himself for what he had done. Why hadn't he told Brody? Why had he left it up to Richard? Brody deserved better than that.

"How could you move away and not even tell me?" Brody said in a soft, defeated voice, his pain apparent.

"I haven't left yet." His tone was soft and inviting, subtly if not subconsciously begging Brody to take the bait and be his knight in shining armor and proclaim his love for him. This was the last opportunity Myles would ever give Brody to tell him that he loved him. Seconds seemed like hour as he waited for an answer.

"But you're planning on it. Why?" Brody didn't take the bait. He had his opportunity and once again missed it. Clearly this was not meant to be. He needed to get away from Brody once and for all, since being together as friends would never allow either of them to find true love. Somewhere along the line, Brody had become Myles' point of comparison for anyone he dated and that wasn't fair anymore. Myles had to go, and he was more resolved more than ever to leave.

He wanted Brody to understand. He really needed to escape the situation, get a fresh start, and become a different person. "Because I don't have a reason to stay here anymore." His voice was sad.

"Am I not a good reason to stay?" Brody's face was filled with hurt and disbelief.

"You tell me." It came more harshly than he intended. Maybe since he knew he was at fault for the way he'd handled the situation or maybe because he knew that being a bit cruel was the only way Brody would understand what he was saying to him.

"Is it the Hunter thing? I already told you that I didn't plan on ruining that for you. How could I know Stone and Hunter were the same person? And afterwards I was only trying to protect you."

"I know that. And I'm not mad anymore. *I'm* the reason I'm leaving. I need to grow up and stop looking for my Prince Charming to come find me."

"That's what I've been saying all along." Brody agreed.

Maybe they were once again on the same page about how he was deluding himself with his search for the perfect man.

"Well then, I agree with you," Myles conceded. Brody was right after all. There was no Prince Charming coming for him, certainly not today and probably not ever.

"Do you really think moving to New York is going to make you happy?" Brody felt completely defenseless.

"It's a start."

"So that's it then?"

He could see that Brody finally understood. Myles had made his decision and was going to stand by it, no matter how difficult it was for him or how badly it hurt.

"I guess so." Myles stood firm with his gaze at Brody, who looked devastated.

Without another word Brody turned and hurried out the door.

Myles knew his friend was badly hurt and needed to leave before either of them made a scene. It was self-preservation. He hoped the wound would heal itself one day.

...

Brody parked outside the go-go bar, walked inside, and took a seat as the dancers performed their perpetual ritual. He ordered a drink and looked around. There were no prospects, at least not anyone who would fill in the emptiness he felt inside. He signed, took out his phone, and launched the Grindr app. A chat window opened with the photo of a guy named Cameron.

"Nice pics," the man said. "Into?"

Brody typed a reply.

"So, want to play?"

Brody stopped and took a moment to consider. What was he doing? More to the point, why was he doing this? He didn't give a shit about any of these guys he was sleeping with. Meeting up with them, fucking, and then leaving never to call again, made him feel worse about himself. This was not the life he wanted. This wasn't where he saw himself at thirty-five. It was time he stopped hiding from himself in the beds of strange men. Brody didn't like who he was anymore, and things had to change.

Then he finished his cocktail and deleted the app from his phone.

The bartender stood in front of him. "Get you another?"

Before he could answer, Richard entered the bar and sat beside him. The bartender left to serve another patron and let them talk. It was clear that Brody was there drowning his sorrows and that his friend had come to his aid.

"I'm mad at you," Brody told him, not in the mood to see anyone, especially Richard.

"I know, but since I'm your only friend now and your partner at work, I figure you need to get over it pretty quickly."

"You knew it was a going away party." His tone was hard, accusatory.

"I'm sorry I didn't tell you, but I thought you deserved to hear it directly from Myles. Plus, if I told you, you wouldn't have come and said goodbye."

"You don't know me." He felt anger churning inside.

"Yeah, it's like we've never met," Richard parried back.

Brody shook his head, realizing he meant well and he had no choice but to forgive him.

"You know, he's right. It's better for both of us that he leaves." Brody attempted to see this from Myles' point of view.

"Well, you certainly know what's best." Richard's voice was slightly mocking, but Brody didn't catch on.

"I'm not like Myles. I'm good with being alone." He knew it was a lie even as he said it. It was like he was trying to convince himself.

"It's true. You're not miserable at all when he's gone." Richard hoped that Brody would catch on to his sarcasm.

"Plus, Myles is a hopeless romantic. All he wants is to be is loved."

"Yeah. So unreasonable," Richard continued in his slightly mocking tone.

"He's also a people pleaser. That's all he thinks about when he's with a guy."

"It's horrible. I can see why guys would hate that."

"Myles is like a penguin. He'll bond with you for life—dependable and trustworthy."

"I'm starting to really hate the guy," Richard playfully answered, surprised that Brody was still being serious about this.

"Could you even imagine if *Myles* and I were together?" Brody tried to wrap his mind around what he considered the most ridiculous of situations, his tone just on the edge of hysterical.

"Not at all. It's crazy to think that two people who care about each other like you two do could ever be in a relationship."

"I know, right? If Myles were the perfect guy for me, don't you think I would have figured it out a long time ago?" Brody was no fool. He wasn't one for subtly that was for sure, but he wasn't so oblivious as to miss out on the perfect man if he had been in his life for over ten years.

"Absolutely. You would never overlook something so obvious for so long."

"Exactly. Myles wants to find a husband. And all I want is for him to be happy." Myles and he were too different to ever be a couple. So maybe he was right; the two of them together was just preventing them from finding their perfect partners. Could it be that Myles was making the right decision in leaving and it was Brody's job as his best friend to let him go?

"Then I guess the only way for that to happen is to remove you from his life," Richard asserted. Brody looked at him in agreement. Richard however was being sarcastic, Brody sincere. Richard decided not to attempt to explain the absurdity of the situation to him. If Brody didn't see it on his own, then he'd never get it. Besides he thought, Myles had spent the last ten years trying to show Brody that he was capable and worthy of finding love. If Myles had failed so miserably at the task, what made Richard think that he would succeed?

CHAPTER NINETEEN

The party was over, and all the farewells had been said. The sun had set and the end of a very long day was finally over. Myles entered his apartment, mostly empty except for the clutter of boxes. Everything was ready for the moving truck in the morning. He picked up a bottle of scotch containing only a splash of liquid. Next to the bottle was a cardboard box labeled "glasses" and taped shut. How did he feel? He didn't quite know. He was eager, even anxious to get going. But there were so many things that tied him to Los Angeles. He closed his eyes and simply stood there and took in the moment.

. . .

Brody entered his apartment, cluttered, as usual, with objects of all sorts seemingly abandoned here and there. It was like the apartment embodied his life. The place was badly in need of cleaning. He eyeballed a half-opened beer. *Damn it to hell,* he thought. Why hadn't he seen this coming? Why hadn't he tried... anything?

. . .

Myles couldn't decide whether or not to open the box and take out a glass. Instead, he lifted the bottle to his lips. This was something Myles would never have done in the past, but this was a new Myles. One with reckless abandon. Why not drink straight from the bottle? As he did, he spied the framed photo Brody had given him ten years earlier. It still hung on the wall where he'd placed it. He raised his glass toward it and decided to toast his old friend one final time before heading to bed. "To Brody. I hope one day you find someone to love."

...

Brody collapsed onto the couch. Near the beer stood the photo of himself and Myles, taken on the day they met. As he reached for the beer in his drunken state, he accidently bumped the picture and knocked it off the table. As he bent to pick it up, he saw the glass of the frame was shattered. Just perfect.

He picked up the photo and looked at it for a moment. What a friend he had in Myles. Someone he'd miss dearly and always cherish. Brody felt that his long-time buddy deserved a final toast to end the evening. Brody eyed the warm half-open beer on top of the shelf and took it in hand. He raised the can to Myles. "I hope someday you find someone to love you," he said, gently placing the frame back where it had been. He took a swig of beer and settled back.

Suddenly, it was daytime and months must have passed. Brody entered his now immaculate apartment. He was in his workout gear. In one hand he held his mail, in the other a healthy fruit juice smoothie. He looked different. Clean, sharp and focused. A new man; a different man than he was before. He dropped his keys into a small dish, set down his elixir, and began to look through the pile of envelopes and papers he'd brought in with him. One particular envelope caught his eye. He opened it and saw it was an invitation. It was to Myles' wedding. At first came shock and then confusion.

Then he found himself at an outdoor wedding, complete with gazebo. Myles, the groom, Diane and Richard all stood before a minister in front of a small crowd seated behind them. Brody and Myles caught each other's gaze, and Myles' face brightened. Brody looked for a seat and found one in the first row. It was Myles' wedding, and he obviously had found the perfect man for him to spend the rest of his life with him. Brody was determined to be happy for him.

The ceremony began. "Dearly beloved," the minister said, "we are gathered together here to join together these two men in holy matrimony. This relationship stands for love, loyalty, honesty, and trust, but most of all for friendship. Before they knew love, they were friends, and it was from this seed of friendship that is their destiny. Do not think that you can direct the course of love... for love, if it finds you worthy, shall direct you.

"It is for this reason; into this holy estate these two persons present now come to be joined. If any person can show just cause why they may not be joined together... let them speak now or forever hold their peace."

Brody desperately wanted to intervene, and yet he remained seated and mute. Myles turned toward him and smiled warmly; it was more than a look welcoming a good friend to his wedding. It appeared more like an invitation to say something. A look that beckoned him to interject and stop him from making a mistake. Richard and Diane joined in that look. All eyes were on Brody and time felt like it stood still. Brody tried to speak up but couldn't. He was strangely paralyzed, his eyes filled with tears. Myles turned away, and the minister continued as if this moment had never happened.

"Do you take this man to love, comfort, honor, and keep in sickness and in health, in sadness and in joy, to cherish and bestow upon him your heart's deepest devotion, as long as you both shall live?"

"I do," Myles answered.

The minister turned to the other man. "And do you take this man to love, comfort, honor, and keep in sickness and in health, in sadness and in joy, to cherish and bestow upon him your heart's deepest devotion, as long as you both shall live?"

"I do," the man replied, his voice oddly familiar.

"Then by the powers vested in me, I now pronounce you husband and husband. You may kiss your groom."

Myles smiled, closed his eyes, and leaned forward to kiss his new husband...This was a man who could finally bring him the happiness he deserved. Brody could see Myles was happy in the union and it was finally

*right. Brody looked closely at Myles' new groom. He instantly and fully
recognized him. He was looking at himself. Myles husband was Brody.*

Suddenly, Brody opened his eyes. He was home on the couch
where he'd passed out after drinking who knew how many beers.

It was morning and Brody had woken a new man, a man who
belonged by Myles' side. Brody was the only person who would
ever be at that altar with Myles. Even if it was only a dream, it felt
right. It felt perfect and he was not going to let anything get in his
way from telling Myles he finally realized that he loved him. That
he'd loved him all along! Almost in a panic, he grabbed his phone
and looked at the date and time. He jumped up and raced outside.
It was late in the morning, and he hoped beyond hope that Myles
hadn't left yet.

. . .

From the doorway Myles gave his apartment one last look. The
photo of him and Brody still hung on the wall. No reason to take
it with him. That part of his life was in the past. He felt sad now
actually to be leaving. He gave the photo one last look as he picked
up the last of the boxes containing his life and made his way out the
door towards his car, where a new beginning awaited him.

CHAPTER TWENTY

Brody rushed out to his car. He lived only a few miles from Myles, but in LA, a few miles could take forever in traffic. Immediately he encountered a nightmare come true. A truck was parked in the street behind him; someone was moving into an apartment and blocking the entire road. Well that didn't matter because the truck was behind him. However, the driver was using a dolly to cart things across the road... in front of him. And he seemed to be in no hurry.

"Damn it!" Brody exploded. He leaned on the horn. Nothing. Why did this have to happen now, of all times? Just then a car came toward Brody, its front bumper stopping only inches from his. He was hemmed in.

An eternity later, or so it seemed, the man got into his truck, backed up, and pulled away. Brody's tires squealed as he reversed in order to then go around the car in front of him. He peeled away from the curb and drove as fast as he could to Myles' apartment building. Jumping from his car, he raced inside and banged on the door. "Myles?" he yelled. "Myles? Are you in there?"

Suddenly, the door across the hall jerked open, and the neighbor stuck his head into the hallway. "What are you goddamn kids up to now?" barked the inquisitive neighbor who was dressed in pajamas and a bathrobe.

"Sorry to disturb you." Brody caught himself realizing he was indeed making quite a racket for this hour of the morning.

"Officer, I didn't realize it was you. Still haven't caught him yet?"

"Have you seen him?" Why not use this snoop to his advantage?

"Saw him this morning. Woke me up making a ruckus. I went back to sleep. Which I never do, by the way. Damn sciatica kept me up all night. Just bought one of the dial mattresses. Changed it from a four to a six. Thought that would help. I slept better on my old Sealy. Think they'd take this one back? It's only been six weeks." Finally, the old man stopped talking. Brody didn't have time for small talk. He needed information and he needed it fast. He was determined to get this guy to actually be of help to him.

"I've got to get to Myles, if you know where he is?"

"Gone now. Looks like you missed him."

"It does." He felt utterly defeated.

"Well you're going after him aren't you?" the neighbor inquired with a glint in his eye.

"He's not a criminal," Brody explained finally.

"I know that! I ain't blind or stupid. You obviously love him," he fired back, surprising Brody. But not as much as Brody's answer surprised himself.

"I do love him." This was the first time Brody said it out loud and it actually felt good to voice it.

"Then you need to go after him. Don't make the same mistake I did and end up like me. Trust me. Don't just stand there. Go after him!"

"I have no idea where he is. He's on his way to New York. I'll never catch up to him."

"You got a cop car, don't you? Light up that son-of-a-bitch. I seen them go over two hundred miles an hour! Tear ass down that freeway!"

Brody just stood there. Could this old coot be right? Richard lived close by and had the cruiser. Should he in fact give chase to Myles?

"For God's sake, man, don't let him get away!"

Brody realized he was right. He wasn't going to let him get away. Brody could do this and he was determined to get Myles back. He thanked the old man and rushed down the stairs to his car.

The neighbor shook his head. "Crazy kids." He gave one last concerned, paranoid look around the courtyard before retreating into his abode.

. . .

Brody rushed to Richard's house to pick up the squad car. He parked and rushed to Richard's apartment where he banged on the door. "Come on, Richard, open up." He banged again. "Come on, I mean it."

Bleary-eyed, Richard appeared in the doorway wearing only his boxers.

"I'm sorry for getting you up so early. But it's Myles. He just left. And we've got to catch him. I need the squad car!"

"Who needs sleep on a Saturday morning?" He could see the passion in Brody's eyes. Brody was on fire and he needed Richard to help him fulfill his romantic quest." It's just like those *Lifetime* movies he and Diane watch." Richard seemed more excited than Brody.

"I've got to catch him before it's too late. Do me a favor and call his phone and see where he is."

"No way! That's not how it's done. Myles is a romantic. You need to catch him. It's the element of surprise that will win him back."

"Are you kidding me?"

"It's all about romance, my friend. You need to catch up to him and tell him how you feel in person."

"What if I don't get to him in time?"

"You always catch up to them! Trust me on this one. I know how it's done. You always get the guy in the end."

"Well, give me the keys to the squad car. I'm going after him!"

"I'm going with you. I'm not about to miss a good chase, especially if it's one that ends in romantic crescendo."

Brody rolled his eyes. Who would believe that this big, tough cop was a hopeless romantic softie?

The two men jumped into the squad car, fired up the lights and siren and sped down the freeway towards the border, intent on finding Myles.

...

The hot morning sun bore down on them as a small brush blew across the desert plain. Brody and Richard stood by their cruiser, just shy of the state line in Nevada wondering where they had gone wrong. They had driven all the way to Nevada with no hint of Myles. He'd done it again, taken Richard's advice!

"Well," Brody said sardonically, "calling him doesn't seem like such a bad idea now, does it?"

"It always works in the movies."

"What do we do now?" He was utterly despondent.

"I don't know. This isn't usually the way it turns out."

Brody slumped against the cruiser. It was time to acknowledge the reality of the situation. "I've lost him, haven't I?" He'd screwed up and he knew it. He'd let Myles get away. All the years and opportunities Myles gave him to love him; he missed every single one of them. And now minutes after Myles' departure, he was ready to commit to a relationship. This was the very definition of a day late and a dollar short.

Richard didn't answer. He knew there was nothing he could say to make his buddy feel better. Brody screwed up. They both knew it and there was nothing now that could be done.

"We might as well go back," Brody said. "Besides, I know you have plans with Diane."

"Yeah. Let me call her and tell her I'll be a little late." He pulled out his phone and dialed. Brody felt he had already ruined two lives today, so why screw things up for Richard and Diane, as well?

...

Diane was putting dishes away when the phone rang. She looked at the caller ID. It was Richard. "This better not be a 'can't-make-it-today' call!" Diane answered.

"No. I'll be there. Small emergency. I'll just be a little late."

"Fine, but hurry so you can start to make it up to me. And don't forget to bring your uniform—especially the night stick." She flirted as she hung up knowing that Richard liked to be teased about a bit of the fun that was to be had when he arrived.

She turned to Myles, who sat at the table. "Richard's going to be late. Keep me company for just a bit more?"

"I really need to be going. I've three thousand miles ahead of me, and now all I'll be able to think about is you and Richard playing 'cops and robbers'."

"You should watch me try to resist arrest," she remarked playfully.

"I really need to hit the road. I just wanted help you clean up and say goodbye again."

"Let's just have a mimosa for the road. No one should head into the middle of this country without at least one drink in them." Diane was being selfish now. She didn't want to see her bestie go. She wanted him to spend a little time with her before Richard came. She knew that she'd be sad when he left, and she wanted him to fill the time before Richard arrived.

Reluctantly, Myles agreed. One drink turned into two and two into three. Heck they were Mimosas–just champagne and orange juice. They weren't strong, and this was the new Myles, a carefree Myles who, unlike the old uptight one, was letting his hair down. What was the rush to get to New York? He'd join her for a bit longer.

CHAPTER TWENTY-ONE

Richard and Brody drove up in front of Diane's house. The plan was to drop Richard off and take the squad car to Richard's where his own car was. It had been a long frustrating morning, and Brody just wanted to go home and be alone. This wasn't something Brody often craved, but he was a different man now. He wanted to examine his feelings, to reflect on what he was going to do with his life. He was determined to figure out where he had gone wrong and was resolved that when he found out, he'd fix it.

"Are you sure you don't want to join us for brunch?"

Brody knew Richard was worried and didn't want to leave him alone today. "You know a gay man is tired when he passes up brunch. I had a bad night and a crappy morning." In fact, he couldn't imagine anything worse than being out with people making light of what he was going through. Brody just wanted to be alone, but Richard wouldn't relent.

"Bottomless drinks. I have a feeling you'll get your money's worth today."

"I'm not really into being around people right now. Especially those in love." He had to be honest with Richard in hopes that he'd let him just go sulk at home by himself. It was like he was channeling Myles now.

Richard started to open the car door when Diane came out and stuck her head though the window.

"Where the hell were you two?" she asked. "Oh you brought the squad car. Nice touch!" Her face lit up at the thought that she and Richard were going to enjoy a little role-play this afternoon.

"We drove to Nevada this morning. We were trying to catch up with Myles."

"Nevada!" She looked puzzled. "Why are you looking for Myles?"

"Brody needs to talk to him. He doesn't want him to leave."

"Well, you missed him."

"Obviously," Brody chimed in, trying not to sound overly obnoxious.

"Talk about detective's instinct. I mean he just left! He was here a minute ago."

"Hey, we can still catch him!" Brody dialed Myles' number. He was done playing with these two and their silly romantic notions on how love works. Brody was in control now and going to do things his way.

"You can't call him," Diane said. "That's not the way it works in the movies!"

"That's what I tried to tell him," Richard said in agreement with her.

Yeah, right, Brody thought, and look how that turned out. He punched Myles' number. There was no answer. In fact, it went directly to voicemail. Either Myles' phone was off, or he didn't want to talk to Brody. Either way, calling was not an option.

Myles, was actually just down the block in his car contemplating what do to do, and wondering if he, in fact, had had too much to drink. Through the rearview mirror he spied Diane and the two men in front of her house. He looked around for a way to escape. It was a cul-de- sac. He'd have to pass in front of Diane's house in order to get away. Myles had only one choice, to try to casually drive by them in hopes that they won't notice. He started his engine and drove down the block. He turned and attempted to quickly drive by.

Suddenly, Diane spotted him. "He's right there!"

Jumping out of the police cruiser and racing as fast as he could, Brody threw himself in front of Myles' car, forcing him to either stop or run over him. Myles slammed on the brakes.

"Are you crazy!" He yelled. "I could have killed you!"

Brody smiled and nodded, as if to acknowledge that indeed he was crazy. But he also wasn't going to move. He had never been happier about anything in his life before, and he was determined not to let Myles get away. He stood leaning against the hood of the car with a stupid grin on his face.

"Move, Brody! Let me go! I refuse to play any more games with you."

"Are you kidding me? Stop, Myles."

"No. Get out of my way!"

Diane and Richard hurried to the front of Myles' car, so the three of them stood there blocking the car so it couldn't reverse or go forward. Myles was trapped inside his BMW mini and had no choice but to get out and face Brody. Diane and Richard both looked at Brody and nodded, giving him permission to go to the side window to lure Myles out.

"Come on. The three of you. I have to leave."

"Myles," Brody demanded.

"No." He stuck his head out the window. He looked toward Richard and Diane, the latter of who had now gone round behind his car so he couldn't back up. "Let me go. Move!"

They both just stood there, arms crossed.

"Don't any of you get it?" Myles said, obviously exasperated and angry. "I can't stay here." He leaned on the horn, but they held their ground. Myles opened the door and stepped out, face filled with frustration. "Why are all of you doing this? There's nothing you can do to make me stay."

Suddenly, Brody grabbed him and kissed him hard.

Myles stepped back, surprised and annoyed. "Was that supposed to change my mind?"

"That was the plan." He was more than a bit confused. Myles didn't react like he had hoped or expected about his revelation.

"Well, it didn't work. I can't do this with you anymore. I have to do what's best for me now, and that's getting away from you." Myles couldn't believe Brody would try to manipulate him like this to try to get him to stay.

It was like a fist punching Brody in the gut. It hurt that much.

"I thought I needed someone to take care of me," Myles continued. "But I don't."

Brody needed to make things right with Myles. He was willing to trust someone again. Open his heart for the first time in a decade. "You may not need someone, but you deserve someone. I want to be that someone." Myles was angry and hurt, he could clearly see it. He was sorry for all the pain he could see in Myles' eyes.

"You're not capable of having a relationship," Myles said sadly. He wished things could be different between Brody and himself, but he knew that couldn't happen. Brody was who he was and that was never going to change.

"So what have we been doing for the last ten years?" His face held a pleading look. "I may not be the Prince Charming you've been looking for, but you know I'd slay a dragon for you." Brody's voice cracked with an honesty that Myles had never heard. His face softened with a glow Myles had never ever seen before. No, actually he did see it once and only once.

It was on Myles' graduation day when he showed Myles the two tickets to Paris he had purchased to Paris to propose to Wayne. He knew then that Brody was being sincere.

Myles' tone became softer. "That's not enough, Brody."

"What more is there?"

"Trust. Companionship. Love. Respect," Myles said.

"Don't we have all those things?"

Myles didn't answer. Brody had him. He thought for a minute, that maybe, just maybe, he was right.

"I'll make it easy on you then. Since you really don't have a choice," Brody asserted, catching Myles off guard once again.

"I'm sorry. What did you just say?"

Brody turned to Diane. "I'm glad you're here because I need a lawyer." He pulled a paper napkin from his pocket. It was the one he and Myles had signed ten years earlier to Myles' utter disbelief.

"I need to know if this is legally binding."

"I charge seven hundred dollars an hour." She paused. "Fine, I'll do it pro bono. Let me see it." Brody handed her the napkin.

Myles couldn't believe his eyes. That was the napkin they had signed ten years earlier. He was convinced that it didn't exist. He was sure Brody either had thrown it away, or he'd left it at the table, dismissing it as a joke between friends. Myles had written off its existence ten years earlier. Now he was shaken to the core to think that not only had Brody saved it for a decade, but he had also carried it and was now planning on using it as a legal document to bind him and Myles together.

Diane glanced at it and shook her head. "I'm sorry to tell you this, but it's not legally binding. It states that it becomes effective on Myles' birthday. That's not until tomorrow."

"I'll have to wait another twelve hours?" Brody asked with a grin.

"We can put him under house arrest until this contract is due," Richard said. "I can leave this perp in your custody." He delivered the line as if he was booking a hardened criminal.

"I'm sorry, but the law's the law," Brody said, eyes filled with pleading.

They all looked at Myles, waiting for a response, which did not come quickly. Myles was frozen in shock. Had Brody finally come around? Was Myles to believe that Brody loved him as he had loved Brody all these years? Was his fairy tale coming true, and was he finally about to be with the man of his dreams? Myles didn't know how to react but one thing for sure, he wasn't going to make it easy on Brody.

"I'm glad you've all made a decision on what I should do," Myles finally said sternly. "Does anyone want to ask me what I think?'

For a moment there was utter silence as Diane, Richard and Brody awaited the verdict from Myles.

"Of course," Brody answered softly.

"I think after waiting ten years, I deserve a proper kiss."

A smile erupted on Brody's face as he reached and grabbed Myles. The two men cemented their new relationship with a long-awaited kiss, a kiss that was ten years in the making. They held each other in their arms and pressed their hearts together. They were finally as one and nothing had ever felt so right as this to either of them. Even Diane and Richard were impressed at this display of affection as they looked at each other.

...

The soft chirp of crickets indicated another warm summer night. Myles lay in his bed completely satisfied. He was a man who now had everything he ever wanted. A big smile crossed his face. *How lucky I am,* he thought.

Suddenly his iPad sprang to life with the sound off his FaceTime ring. Who could be calling him at this hour? Only one person he could think of. He rolled over to see Brody's toothy grin staring at him on the screen. With a swipe of his finger, he answered. "And you're calling me why?" he asked, knowing full well the reason.

"I always call you after I hook up with a hot guy," he chuckled coquettishly.

"Well, how was it?"

"Let me put it this way. I'm going to have to call you back. I'm about to do it again."

"That good?" Myles asked, again knowing full well the answer.

"Oh, yes!" He paused. "And by the way, Myles, happy birthday."

"It certainly is." Myles answered as he looked next to him in the bed where Brody smiled back at him, obviously pleased at his own cleverness as he held his phone with Myles Face-Timing on it. They looked at each other in a long loving gaze and hung up their respective devices. They had come full circle and now had what they both always wanted but were too blind to see.

As if the movements were choreographed, the two shirtless men rolled toward each other and kissed. Deeply, passionately. They'd finally consummated their love for each other and were about to do it again.

This was by far Myles' best birthday ever, and the final chapter of their ten-year plan.

On Myles' nightstand near them lay the napkin containing the ten-year plan and next to it stood the framed photo of the two of them on the day they first met.

THE END

MYLES' FAVORITE RECIPES

Food is one of the best ways to show and share love. Myles loves to create wonderful meals for his dates in an attempt win their hearts. Here are some of his favorites for you to enjoy and share with your loved ones.

Eggplant Sorrento (Kodi's Mom's Recipe)
Thanks to Kodi's Mom for sharing this family recipe with Myles so he could prepare it on their special date.

Chocolate-Covered Strawberries Infused with Cognac (Date Night Special)
What man is sexier than a man eating a strawberry covered in chocolate? Just wait till a little trickles down the side of his cheek. There's only one way to clean that up -- with a kiss.

Myles' Homemade Tiramisu Recipe (Guaranteed to Win a Man's Heart)
The last step before whisking him away to the boudoir. What's better than an authentic Italian dessert? Nothing says amore like Tiramisu.

French Onion Soup (Myles' Guilty Pleasure)
Eat only when feeling blue! This always cheers Myles up after being dumped or stood up! Don't forget the baguettes with lots of butter!

Pan-seared Steak au Poivre (Dad's Favorite)

This always put a smile on Dad's face when Myles was growing up. (Just don't tell Mom Myles is cooking behind her back again!) Myles still credits this meal as the reason his father paid his tuition.

EGGPLANT SORRENTO

Ingredients:

2 medium sized eggplant (each eggplant makes approx. 6-8
   slices)
1 bag frozen spinach
1 clove garlic
All purpose flour – 1 cup
Marinara or a la Vodka sauce – 1 cup
Garlic powder
Vegetable oil
Salt and pepper
2 eggs
5 oz Parmesan cheese
8 oz Mozzarella cheese
2 cups Italian flavored breadcrumbs
2 pork sausages skin removed

Servings:
Serves 2-4

Directions:
   • Using Black Eggplants, cut off both ends, cut eggplants
      vertically (lengthwise), remove ends piece and discard

- Slice eggplant leaving skin on outer edges – slices should be approximately 1/8 of inch, place in colander
- Salt between each slice, this helps to remove any bitterness
- Cover with wax paper and place a weight on top to apply pressure
- Let stand for approximately one hour, rinse salt off, dry with paper towels

- Place all purpose flour in flat dish, then in a separate bowl add the eggs (whisked) and salt, in a third bowl place Italian flavored breadcrumbs
- Dip the eggplant slices in flour, then shake excess flour off
- Dip the floured breaded eggplant in egg
- Dip the **eggplant slice** in flavored breadcrumbs
- Press breadcrumbs slightly to make sure they adhere
- Transfer to paper towel

- In heavy skillet add approximately ½ inch of vegetable or peanut oil, heat oil until hot, and fry eggplant until each is golden brown
- Transfer to paper towel to drain excess oil from eggplant

- Set aside

Note: Eggplant absorbs oil while cooking, replenish oil as necessary.

- In large frying pan, sauté oil and garlic (cut into small pieces) until garlic is golden brown
- Add two links of sausage (out of casing) using the meat only
- Stir until browned
- Add package of thawed frozen chopped spinach to mixture (press out excess water of spinach once it's thawed)

- Add salt, pepper, garlic powder, as well as 5 Tbsp of grated cheese while stirring mixture
- After mixture is cooled add diced mozzarella

- In a 10 square inch baking pan, place breaded eggplant with spinach and sausage mixture rolled into cylinder shape (seam down in pan)
- Cook in oven approximately 15 minutes
- Top with a vodka sauce or tomato marinara sauce
- Top with mozzarella cheese and bake until it melts (an additional 10 minutes)

Note: Marinara sauce is oil, garlic fresh tomatoes chopped or can of tomatoes, cayenne pepper (optional) salt and pepper, fresh basil. Vodka Sauce or Marinara can be bought prepared.

CHOCOLATE-COVERED STRAWBERRIES INFUSED WITH COGNAC

Ingredients:
1 lb (about 20) strawberries with stems, washed and dried very well
6 oz semisweet chocolate, chopped

Directions:
- Rinse, but do not hull the strawberries
- Drain and pat completely dry

- With a cooking syringe inject cognac, Grand Marnier or your favorite liquor into strawberries

- Put the semisweet chocolate into heatproof medium bowls
- Fill medium saucepan with a couple inches of water and bring to a simmer over medium heat
- Turn off the heat and set the bowls of chocolate over the water to melt
- Stir until melted and smooth
- Remove from the heat
- Line a sheet pan with parchment or waxed paper

Note: Alternatively, melt the chocolates in a glass dish in the microwave on high power for 60 seconds. Remove, stir and microwave for 10 seconds more until the chocolate has melted. Allow the chocolate to cool slightly to thicken.

- Holding the strawberry by the stem, dip the bottom half of each strawberry in the melted chocolate
- Twist the strawberry so that the chocolate forms a "tail" at the end
- Set strawberries on the parchment paper

MYLES' HOMEMADE TIRAMISU RECIPE

Ingredients:

1 cup heavy whipping cream

Half cup prepared coffee

1 double shot espresso

1 lb mascarpone cheese

Half cup granulated sugar

3 Tbsp rum or brandy

20 ladyfingers (a light, oblong Italian cookie with powdered sugar on one side)

Cocoa powder

1 oz unsweetened dark chocolate shavings

Directions:

- Chill whipping cream and bowl of electric mixer (or standard metal mixing bowl)
- Mix coffee and espresso and chill

- Whisk the whipping cream until it reaches stiff peaks - this can be accomplished in a few minutes with an electric mixer or by hand, times will vary depending on arm strength and stamina

- Put the cheese, sugar, and brandy into a medium bowl and mix until smooth

- Add more sugar or alcohol as desired

- Fold in the whipped cream to create the cheese mixture

- Dip the ladyfingers in espresso for a couple seconds, rotating to coat all sides
- Place ladyfingers side by side on bottom of a 8-by-8-inch pan

- Put half the cheese mixture on ladyfingers
- Smooth with a spatula or spoon
- Sift cocoa powder liberally on surface of layer

- Apply second layer of lady fingers and remaining cheese
- Sift cocoa powder and half of chocolate shavings
- Cover in plastic wrap and chill

To serve, use the remaining chocolate shavings by sprinkling a bit onto eight plates. Cut tiramisu into eight rectangles and serve on plates (or simply spoon them out).

FRENCH ONION SOUP

Ingredients:

6 Tbsp unsalted butter

4 lbs onions (about 6 medium), thinly sliced

Kosher salt and black pepper

1 cup dry white wine

2 cups low-sodium beef broth

8 1/2-inch-thick slices country bread, halved crosswise if necessary
   to Fit serving bowls

2 cups grated Gruyere or Swiss cheese

1 Tbsp fresh thyme leaves

Time 120 minutes / Serves 8

Directions:
- Heat the butter in a large pot over medium-high heat
- Add the onions, 1¼ salt, and ¼ Tsp pepper and cook, covered, stirring occasionally, until tender, 12 to 15 minutes
- Reduce heat to low and cook, uncovered, stirring occasionally, until the onions are golden brown, 50 to 60 minutes

- Add the wine and cook until slightly reduced, about 2 minutes
- Add the broth and 6 cups water and bring to a boil
- Reduce heat and simmer for 15 minutes

- Meanwhile, heat broiler
- Place the bread on a broiler-proof baking sheet and broil until golden brown and crisp, 1 to 2 minutes per side then sprinkle with the cheese and broil until melted, 1 to 2 minutes

- Divide the soup among bowls, top with the toasts, and sprinkle with the thyme

PAN-SEARED STEAK AU POIVRE

Ingredients:

4 small filet mignons, 1-inch thick
1 Tbsp cracked black peppercorns
1 Tbsp olive oil
1/2 cup beef broth
1/4 cup cognac (optional)
2 Tbsp butter, cut into 4 pieces

Time 15 minutes / Serves 4

Directions:

- Pat each filet mignon dry with paper towels, then sprinkle each side with the pepper

- Heat a heavy skillet, preferably cast iron, on the stovetop over medium-high heat until a few drops of water dance across the surface

- Add the oil, then the steaks, and cook 3 to 4 minutes, adjusting the heat as necessary so the oil stays hot but does not smoke

- Turn the steaks and cook until small drops of red juice come to the surface, about 5 minutes for medium
- Transfer to a platter and keep warm

- Add the broth to the skillet over high heat and scrape up any browned bits
- Pour in the cognac (if desired) and boil 1 to 2 minutes to burn off the alcohol

- Remove the skillet from the heat and whisk in the butter, one piece at a time, until melted
- Pour the sauce over the steaks

BRODY'S RULES TO LIVE BY

1. Appreciate and accept yourself. Be good with who you are.

2. Just like in bed - if you like it done to you- they'll like it done to them. Be as generous as possible. You need to give in order to get.

3. Nothing is more attractive than confidence. Don't play coy or play games.

4. Don't spend money on fancy stuff. Expensive stuff is a waste of money. Buy affordable, quality goods. No one needs $300 jeans. Nothing is as sexy as a pair of $40 Levis.

5. Nothing is sexier than a man who is smart. Speak well and be informed. Education is hot.

6. Be honest. Liars always get caught. It takes time and energy trying to remember stories that aren't true. No one wants to be with a liar.

7. Don't complain or talk badly about other people. No one wants to listen to someone bitch and moan or talk about other people.

8. Push yourself. Try new things. Be someone who is exciting and always exploring new stuff.

9. Enjoy today. Do something that will make you happy.

10. Stop caring what others think of you. If you're okay with it, then that's the way it is.

11. No one likes to be with a bummer. Have fun – be the person people want to be around.

12. Embrace your generous nature. Give freely and others will give to you in return.

13. Own your shortcomings. Don't make excuses for all the things you aren't. Either fix them or accept them as part of who you are.

14. Surround yourself with good people. Your circle should consist of awesome friends.

15. Remove people from your circle who don't fit the qualities listed above. Why would you want to hang out with people who bring you down?

16. Forgive those who have wronged you in the past. Let it go, learn from it and move on to a better place.

A LETTER FROM THE AUTHOR

Dear Reader,

I find nothing more fascinating than love. Why do people fall in love? What is it like to be in love? What makes you love one person and not the other? Questions like that keep me up at night. Other than being obsessed with love, I enjoy telling a good story. There are many stories out there, but of course my favorite are those about falling in love. I'm a big softy. My partner teases me since I could get teary at a Pepsi commercial. Stories that re-unite people turn me into a ball of mush. These feelings connect us.

I guess that's why out of all professions I could have pursued, being a storyteller is the one that makes me the happiest. Connecting people with their emotions, exploring thoughts that are universal to us, and certainly making us feel all warm, happy and tingly inside. Romantic comedy is the perfect book and movie genre as far as I'm concerned. They show the best in a person as well as the worst but always end with the promise that everything will work out for the best in the end.

As a gay man, my work creates a world that I hope we can all live in – one of total acceptance. Of course, I know ignorance and bigotry exist, but in my stories, we have evolved beyond that. My stories take place where our protagonists are dealing with the universal problems that we all face as people, which is to find and/or keep love. It's not about gay, straight or bi love. It's about love between people. Male or female, trans or otherwise. I hope to create a place where we can recognize the universal truths about ourselves and those who we hope to be with. Prejudice doesn't exist in my world. Hopefully these stories will set an example of how things can be in the real world if we just learn to look past the biases we've been taught to have and learn that love is love - regardless of how you couple the sexes.

The 10 Year Plan is my third story of the exploration of love. The first *Is It Just Me?* explores self-love and acceptance and the idea of being good enough and deserving of the man of your dreams. My second film *eCupid* investigates the "seven year itch". I believe that often in a relationship one, if not both, of the partners wonder "is this the person I want to be with - forever?" *The 10 Year Plan* delves into the question "what's the difference between friendship and love?"

It's based on my life and my two best friends. The idea came about fifteen years ago while we were all out drinking. The real life "Myles" and "Brody" made the exact same 10 year plan as in the film: to be a couple if both of them were still single in ten years. I chuckled to myself, thinking how perfect they both were for each other and how ridiculous it was that they would wait a decade before actually doing something about it.

True to form, 10 years later and the arrangement almost due, each asked me privately about what they should do. They cared for each other deeply but both felt it was unwise to start a romantic relationship. They didn't want to hurt each other's feelings by backing out.

Their predicament made me wonder about the line between friendship and love. Love is certainly friendship, but what makes one relationship plutonic and another romantic? I still don't know the answer, but it was great fun exploring it in writing the *The 10 Year Plan*.

I've come to discover that such back-up plans are relatively common. My cousin reminded me that I made a pact with her when we were kids. We were very close growing up and agreed that if we never found someone to love us, we could always depend on each other.

Enjoy!

- JC

DISCOVER MORE BY JC CALCIANO

Laugh-out-loud funny and seductively sweet, *Is It Just Me?* is a gay romantic comedy about one gay boy's search for Mr. Right. Adorable Blaine, (Nicholas Downs) can't seem to meet guys, let alone form a relationship. His beefy go-go boy roommate Cameron, who has no shortage of willing partners, can't understand why he doesn't just pounce and enjoy some one-nighters.

Instead, Blaine hides in chat rooms where he meets Zander, a shy, recently relocated Texan. But when the time comes to exchange photos, Blaine accidentally sends an image of his hunky roomie, and things go from romantically promising to downright confusing. Full of witty charm and cute guys, *Is it Just Me?* is a bona fide feel-good winner!

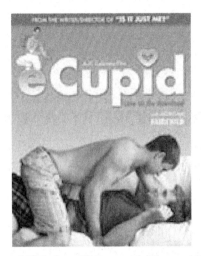

From the director of *Is It Just Me?* comes this sparkling romantic comedy that takes online dating to the extreme! Marshall is an overworked ad exec who is suffering from a serious case of the seven-year itch with his loving boyfriend. As his 30th birthday nears, he is hell-bent on changing his life and he comes across a mysterious dating app called *eCupid*. Turning his world upside down and overwhelming him with sexy, horned-up guys at every turn, Marshall gets much more than he bargained. Firing on all cylinders with sharp wit, hot cast, and even an extended cameo from Hollywood legend Morgan Fairchild, *eCupid* will win your heart.

IMAGES FROM THE MOVIE
THE 10 YEAR PLAN

"The Photo"

Strawberries Dipped in Chocolate

Myles' First Time on Grinder

Myles' Hook-up with Hunter

Movie Night at Diane's

Brody Sleeps with Stone

Brody's Tough Night

Myles Leaves Brody Behind

Richard and Brody Reach Nevada

Happily Ever After

ABOUT THE AUTHOR

JC Calciano has worked as a film producer for 25 years and has worked in various capacities on films such as: *Mission: Impossible, The Fisher King, Star Trek,* and others. When not working on features, JC worked as a writer/producer/director on a great many television programs. After 25 years of producing professionally, his mid-life crisis kicked in. He realized that although he loved producing, the dream that had originally brought him into the film business was to write and direct. JC stopped producing and started writing.

At 45 years old, he wrote his first feature film, *Is It Just Me?* (2010) It was his first film as a writer and director. It was an over-night hit and became the official selection of over 50 international film festivals and won several awards and honors, including audience choice and best picture. From that point on, he was hooked. He had the writing bug and set forth to make another film.

JC's second feature film, *eCupid* (2012), became another best seller in the LGBTQ market and won four best picture and audience choice awards.

His newfound passion for romantic comedy films, as well as the desire to tell the story of his best friends' semi-romantic tryst, inspired him to write his third feature film, *The 10 Year Plan* (2015). The film was screened at over 51 international film festivals and winner of 10 awards for best feature and screenplay. *The 10 Year Plan* screenplay was selected as a finalist in the Rainbow Literary

Awards. This honor inspired JC to write the screenplay into a novel for those who enjoy reading rather than watching a film.

This book is JC's first novel and his faithful adaptation of the screenplay and movie of the same name. He hopes that you enjoy the book as much as the audience has enjoyed the movie.

To learn more about JC Calciano and his work go to: JcCalciano. com

CPSIA information can be obtained
at www.ICGtesting.com
Printed in the USA
LVOW13ᴇ2052230617

539169LV00009B/492/P